SEED OF EVIL
GREIG BECK

SEVERED PRESS
HOBART TASMANIA

SEED OF EVIL

Copyright © 2021 GREIG BECK
Copyright © 2021 by Severed Press

WWW.SEVEREDPRESS.COM

All rights reserved. No part of this book may be reproduced or transmitted in any form or by any electronic or mechanical means, including photocopying, recording or by any information and retrieval system, without the written permission of the publisher and author, except where permitted by law.
This novel is a work of fiction. Names, characters, places and incidents are the product of the author's imagination, or are used fictitiously. Any resemblance to actual events, locales or persons,
living or dead, is purely coincidental.

ISBN: 978-1-922551-62-7

All rights reserved.

*"Destroy the seed of evil,
or it will grow up to your ruin."*
– Aesop

"The tree of life was always there."
– Simon Conway Morris, British scientist

PROLOGUE

Circa 12,000 BC – what will one day become Missouri

In the cool, silver light of the full moon, the tribe watched silently as the captives were led up the stony hill to the cave entrance.

The men and women were taken during a raiding party on a distant tribe, and the chief stared blankly as the procession moved by him—men, women, and youths, all roped together with hands lashed behind their backs.

Every time the lake was swallowed by the cave after the ground shook, they needed their human stocks refilled, and they scouted out the other tribes for this precious resource.

Many wept, some still looked in shock, and a few glared back defiantly. The chief might have felt some twinge of guilt, but he knew that their god needed to be sated, and if it wasn't these souls, then it would be his people.

At the cave mouth, one lashed man dragged the group to a stop and yelled back about angering his tribe's god and ancestors and vowed to curse them to eternity.

The chief grunted and turned away when the last of them was jerked into the impenetrable darkness of the cave. It didn't matter to the chief about curses and offending other deities. Because the difference between other gods and his god was that his god was real.

And their lands were already cursed.

PART 1 – A NEW BEGINNING

CHAPTER 01

Syria, Idlib Province – Kurdish evacuation – 8 years ago

Captain Mitch Taylor and his team crouched as heavy machinegun fire tore up the ground just out to their left flank.

Another day in paradise, he thought.

Mitch had spent three years in med school before heeding the call and enlisting. His medical work was put on hold while he had thrown himself into his military training. He exceled and eventually tried out for Special Forces selection, where he succeeded first try. Mitch was a trained killer of evil, but if called upon, he could also heal.

A mortar exploded 100 feet from them, and he turned his head away from the falling debris. He and a few dozen Special Forces were on the ground in Idlib to assist in creating a safe corridor for the trapped Kurdish and Syrian refugees. But it was turning out to be a near-impossible task.

He lifted his head; in front of him, a few of the Kurdish YPG hunkered down, and one of them, Aiisha, turned to smile broadly back at him.

She was like a lot of the Kurdish women who fought alongside their men; they were as fearless as they were ferocious, and after he'd saved her brother's life, she seemed to have decided she either owed him something or he was now future husband material.

"*Fuck.*"

Another mortar exploded, closer. He knew the Syrian army was finding their range and they were running out of time.

"They're on us; we need to pull back," his buddy, Henson, yelled to him.

He waved him down. "Not yet; we can do it."

Mitch should have pulled them back, but he knew that nothing was achieved without risk. And what he needed to do would save hundreds. Mitch shook his head.

"We push through, get under it."

Where they were was described as a blood and bone salad—there were Syrian forces, Russian Special Forces, Kurdish YPG, ISIS, Hezbollah, Al Qaida, and too many other small factions to name, all of them armed to the teeth, and all killing, screaming, and dying in equal measures.

It was no place to be a refugee, and that was why he and his unit, *the Asgardian Shields*, were on the ground. It was a near hopeless task, and he knew that the reward for doing impossible tasks, and succeeding, was just being handed more impossible tasks.

They had one more sniper nest to take down, and then they could begin bringing the people through. Mitch and two of his Special Forces buddies moved up to join the small group of YPG.

It was agreed Mitch and his guys would draw enemy attention and lay down supressing fire while Aiisha and her team would advance, and then more than likely throw themselves head-first into an enemy foxhole with gun in one hand and blade in the other. This place was a mad world.

Their plans were set, and she turned to smile at him again and put a finger to her lips, and then turned the finger to face him for a moment before making a fist. He nodded and smiled in return—it meant: *this kiss for you, I keep it 'til we meet again.*

His buddies weren't watching so he did the same back. Okay, he admitted it—he liked her too.

He allowed their groups to split and Aiisha's team advanced 50 feet, all the time staying low. But it was then that the back of Mitch's neck prickled. Around him, the air became still and everything dropped away to silence. Whether it was a soldier's intuition, or a premonition, he knew something was coming. And it was something bad.

Suddenly, he also knew for sure—*he shoulda pulled them back*. It was as if the very air became thick like honey and time slowed down. Specks of dirt seemed to float, burning cinders hung like tiny lights in the smoke-filled air, and open mouths roared things that weren't words anymore.

Mitch could only stare as the Russian-heavy mortar,

probably an M240 that fired a 286-pound shell, landed in the center of Aiisha and her group. The percussive blast blew a crater 40 feet around, and he was lifted and thrown backward to roll like a broken doll until he struck a rocky outcrop.

He remembered his face feeling hot and wet, and the flesh sizzling like steak on the grill while even as his eyes burned and his eardrums screamed, he could still hear the moans of the obliterated and dying around him.

"*Don't leave them, don't leave them.*" There was the salty taste of blood in his mouth as he yelled when hands grabbed his torn and battered body and dragged him away.

He didn't know who it was that pulled him out of there. But his military days were over, and Aiisha, and everyone else he knew, were gone forever.

CHAPTER 02

Eldon, Oakland County, Missouri – Today

Michael 'Mitch' Taylor pulled to the side of the road and checked his map. Somewhere around here was his turnoff, but he found country roads were like his mother's pet parakeets—they were beautiful, but they all looked the same to him. For all Mitch knew, he had been going in circles for hours.

He wound down the window and inhaled the smell of drying grass and wild flowers, and listened to the *zumm* of cicadas and crickets. He smiled. *A new start*, he thought.

He was still only 35 years old but felt like he had already lived two lifetimes—the first was a military life. There, he'd seen more blood and horror to last forever.

He fucked up, made a bad call, and when he had finally woken up in a hospital all those years ago with his face covered in bandages and his body feeling like it was beaten to a pulp, he felt lucky. He would heal, but Aiisha and most everyone else there that day had either ceased to exist in one loud and pulverizing flash or lay there broken and dying as he was extracted.

He knew they must have all been obliterated, but deep in his soul were the scars of guilt because he might just have left them behind.

Mitch was honorably discharged and then embarked on his next life, the civilian one. He had gone back to college to finish his medical degree and there he met Cindy, and suddenly his life became full of color, light, laughter, and love again.

In eight months, they were married and living in a big city; he working as a general medical practitioner, and she in a downtown law firm. Their lives were stable, quiet, and looking like it'd make for a pretty damn good future for them. They even talked about kids—one each, a boy and a girl.

But shit luck seemed to follow him like a dark cloud. Because then Cindy got *the lump*. He had told her not to worry as she went in for further tests. But secretly he had been scared to death, and when she got the results back, she handed him all the lab reports and looked up at him with glistening eyes that held a plea that his medical knowledge would somehow translate the horrible truth on the pages into something it wasn't.

Instead, one glimpse at the dense mass-network in the images and the accompanying medical notes and he had felt his world begin to crumble under his feet—it was stage 4 breast cancer, metastasized, and inoperable, and that little lump had probably been working its way backward into and right throughout her body for years.

He cried. She grew worse and the treatments just made her last months on Earth unbearable. He cried longer and harder when she finally left him. *Left him*. He scoffed softly at the expression, as he still couldn't bear to say: *she died*.

Even now, years later, sitting in that car by himself, he felt his vision swim once more with tears. *Everyone I love dies*, he thought morosely.

He had wanted to kill himself, had nightmares, drank hard and hit rock bottom, and as he still had his Glock 19, many times he'd pulled it out and just held it as he stared off into the distance, seeing nothing but an endless blankness.

His shrink had recommended a new start as depression was winning the tug-of-war for his mind. And that was where life number three came in—Eldon.

Over breakfast one day, he saw the ad: a small town in Oakland County named Eldon was looking for a family practice doctor. He applied and after several online interviews, more grueling than he expected, and then a FaceTime chat over the internet where he met Keith Melnick, the mayor; Karen Powell, vice mayor, who was young but sharp as a razor; Ralph Gillespie, the town attorney and oversized loudmouth; plus several of the other council members, he had gotten the job.

And now here he was on his way.

Or soon would be. Mitch took a hand from the wheel and wiped his eyes with his forearm.

"A new start." He nodded. "Yep."

He cleared his throat and then pulled out onto the road to set off again.

*****

The ancient Native American lowered his hands as his chant died away. He stood stone-still for several moments and seemed to be listening for something. After a while, he grunted softly and began to pack away his charms, small drum and beater, and herbs into a large cloth bag.

He straightened; his task was done, and the drawing spell was working as he sensed the warrior approaching. He then walked slowly down the dry, scrabbly path from the mine mouth and arrived at the road, looking toward the east.

He had a long way to go before he was home. But he knew that what was coming, would mean he'd soon be back.

CHAPTER 03

In another fifteen minutes of sunny, tree-lined roads, and fields of long grass dotted with stands of silver maple, ash, and oak trees, he saw the sign—*Eldon, Oakland County, population: 1024*—and a turnoff.

Then in another few minutes more, he started to see houses, then more houses, and then he entered Eldon town central. He smiled as he slowed down, delighted it looked exactly like its pictures.

He felt as if he just traveled back to a time and place where people smiled and waved at each other, the streets were wide, and the sun shone on every corner of the world.

He noticed someone behind a window watching him, and gave a small wave, but the curtains were quickly tugged closed. *Well, maybe not everyone smiled and waved.*

He chuckled. "Damn outta towners."

Mitch pulled in close to the council chambers just across from the local museum. He had been given a few contact names—Karen, the vice mayor; Shelly, his soon-to-be assistant nurse; and Doctor Ben Wainright, 79 years old, looking to retire, and why he was here.

There were no parking meters and no street signs, which made his grin even broader; this was definitely an advantage over big cities where cars were seen as the enemy and parking them was a luxury for the rich or the lucky.

He looked across the street. "Vice Mayor Karen first it is then." He shouldered open his door and crossed the near-empty street to the chambers. It was a square 1960-ish building that was one of the few that was totally painted white.

Mitch headed directly to the woman at the front desk beside an oak staircase that could have come straight from the set of Gone with the Wind.

"Hiya." He gave the receptionist his most charming smile.

She returned his smile, crinkle-winked with both eyes, and held up a finger as she finished her phone call.

She disconnected and looked up. "Doctor Taylor." It wasn't a question and her eyebrows traveled halfway up her forehead.

"Guilty." Mitch held his hands up but was still a little surprised that she recognized him.

"I'm Gladys, and we've been expecting you." She beamed like a schoolgirl. "You're as nice as in your pictures. Like a young Ben Affleck."

"Thank you—just don't tell Ben Affleck." Mitch chuckled. "*Ah*, is the vice mayor in?"

"Yes, but she might still be in a meeting. I'll check if she's free." Gladys pressed a button on her phone system, spoke softly for a second or two, and then turned to nod to him. "You're in luck, she's coming down."

An upstairs door opened and closed, and then came the click of heels on linoleum. For some reason, Mitch automatically sucked in his stomach.

Karen Powell came down the steps, her dark eyes on him, and she didn't smile until she stepped down to be right in front of him. First thing he noticed was that in person she was tiny, standing no more than around five feet four inches, give-or-take. The next thing he noticed was she almost seemed luminous, at least to him.

Take it easy, big guy, he thought as he felt his cheeks redden.

She held out her hand. "Doctor Taylor, pleased to meet you in person. Online meetings are so impersonal."

"Thank you, and likewise." He shook her hand and found that though her hand was small, her grip was firm. Also, rather than the soft skin he expected, the palms seemed a little calloused. *Gym junky, or maybe works a large property*, he wondered.

She tilted her head. "So, you found our little oasis without problem?"

He grinned. "Yes, and Eldon is as beautiful as I expected, and it's my pleasure to be here, Vice Mayor. Oh, and please call me Mitch."

"Only if you call me Karen." She watched him. "Just popping in to say hello, or is there something I can do for you?"

"Just on my way to meet with Doc Wainright and let him

know I've arrived. As I was passing by, I wondered if you were in."

"Good," she said. "You'll like Ben, he's been my family doctor for years. As he's retiring soon, I guess I'll be seeing you in the future."

"You and the family?" he asked.

She bobbed her head. "Yes, but it's just me and Benji—Benjamin, my twelve-year-old son."

He waited for a few seconds for her to elaborate but she didn't, so he just assumed it was too early for him to know those sorts of private details. "Okay, great." Mitch waited a moment more and then jerked a thumb toward the door. "So, I better, *ah*, get going then."

She continued to watch him with that small smile of hers before suddenly having a thought. "Hey, this weekend the mayor is having a send-off for Ben, so you're here at the perfect time. Be worthwhile you coming along, meet all your prospective customers."

"Okay, yeah, sounds real good." He gave her a small bow and quickly glanced at Gladys who was on the phone but still watching him. "See you, Gladys."

She crinkled her eyes again and this time her nose as well, while carrying on with her cheery phone conversation.

Back in his car, he read the street sign of the closest cross street to get his bearings. It was Friday and he had planned on checking out his practice on the weekend but found that Wainright's clinic wasn't that far away. He could drop in on the old boy first, and then if he needed any supplies—food and medicines—before opening mid-week, he still had the afternoon to get everything sorted.

He pulled out and headed down the street to the first turnoff at Dugdale Street. Then he motored on past antique shops, general stores, and a few empty coffee shops. Finally, he came to a neat little house with a brass plate out front: *Ben B. Wainright— Medical Practitioner*.

*****

The ground shook.
Just a little.

And anyone out walking might have just thought it was a truck going by. Or their imagination. But the local pigeon flocks took to the sky, and kept on going.

*****

"This must be the place," Mitch said as he pulled over. He sat in the car for a moment admiring the small cottage that was painted in deep blue, with gloss white for the fencing and balustrades. It looked well maintained and it was obvious that Wainright took pride in its upkeep.

Always a good sign, he thought.

He stepped out of his car and smiled. "Mitch, my boy, one day all of this will be yours."

He strode up to the gate and pushed it open. The spring-hinge groaned a little, but then eased itself closed behind him as he walked to the open doorway. He stepped inside the reception area and smelled lavender and alcohol.

Behind the desk, a young woman had her head down with earphones in. Mitch assumed she was transcribing medical notes for Doctor Wainright, but as he neared her desk, he heard the pop music leaking out from the ear plugs and saw she had a magazine open.

He leaned on the counter. "Shelly Horton, I presume?"

She looked up, and her eyes suddenly went from bored to alert. She flapped the magazine shut and flashed him a brilliant smile as she pulled the plugs from her ears.

"Hi there, sorry, can I help you?"

"I think so." Mitch smiled back, even though he didn't like the idea of his potential new receptionist ignoring patients; he guessed if the practice was quiet, then he could cut her some slack.

"I'm Doctor Michael Taylor; is Doctor Wainright about?"

She rose to her feet. "Michael, Doctor Wainright, yes, yes, he is." She stuck out a hand and leaned forward over the desk counter, making the front of her uniform strain. "I'm your receptionist, Shelly Horton."

"Nice to meet you, Shelly." He shook her hand and she held on. "Pretty quiet, *huh*?"

She nodded vigorously, still holding onto his hand and

coming around the desk. "Some days, yes. The Eldon folk here are generally a pretty healthy bunch. Unless it's flu season."

"Well, that's no good." He grinned and eased his fingers free. "How am I supposed to make a living if no one ever needs a doctor?"

She giggled, and her eyes flashed at him. She pointed one slim finger toward a side door. "Would you like me to get him? Doctor Wainright?"

"Sure. I just arrived so I'm only popping in to say hello for now."

"Then *hello*." She waved with both hands and smiled broadly. "I'll wake him up." She headed to the consulting room door and leaned closer as she rapped twice. "Doctor Wainright?"

"*Come.*"

The voice was deep but weary, and Shelly waved him on as she pushed open the door. She poked her head around to check and whisper to Wainright, and then held the door wide.

As Mitch stepped inside, Wainright rose to his feet. He was slim, stooped, and slightly grey-faced, with a thin, aristocratic nose. But his smile was warm, and though slightly rounded at the shoulders now, Mitch bet that once the 79 year old would have been a tall and striking man.

Mitch crossed to him quickly. "Ben, so nice to meet you face to face at last."

"Likewise," Wainright said, shaking his hand. The hand and fingers were soft, and the bones felt like sticks under the papery skin. He stood there examining Mitch for a few seconds more before releasing his hand.

"I'm glad you came." He stared into Mitch's face as his smile fell away to become a deadpan expression. "Mitch, everything I did here, I did for the benefit of the Eldon community." He straightened his narrow shoulders. "But I guess history will be my judge."

Mitch frowned a little. "I, *ah*, think it'll be the judge of all of us."

Wainright grunted and turned to his room. "Just tidying up some redundant files for you."

Mitch saw that there were neat piles of folders and filing cabinets hanging open. All except one; tucked away in a corner was an older wooden cabinet, solid, and the only one with a padlock on it.

Ben saw where he was looking. "Don't worry about that one, as I plan on cleaning it up later. It's just historical information about something that happened here nearly half a century ago."

"The Angel Mine?" Mitch guessed.

Wainright's head whipped around for him to stare again. After another moment, he simply nodded once.

"Yeah, the mine disaster." Mitch shrugged. "I read about it. A dark day. The mine flooded; quite a few deaths, wasn't there?"

"There were indeed. But that was in 1908." Ben turned watery eyes on him. "But this was a localized event from the seventies; just some details of residual cases of skin irritations and other things from the mining chemicals of the day still hanging around. Nothing important."

"I understand there was some resulting affliction called Angel Syndrome," Mitch pressed, recollecting a few references when he was doing his research on Eldon. But there was no real description of what that even meant. "I'd be happy to look it over, just to…"

"*No.*" Wainright's voice cut across him. "It's done with now."

Mitch raised his eyebrows. "No big deal." He turned back to look at the old cabinet again.

"We should have blown that damn mine up," Wainright muttered.

"*Huh?*" Mitch turned back, not sure he heard right, but Wainright waved it away, signaling the conversation was closed.

"This way, Doctor."

"You never told me, Ben," Mitch asked, deciding to change the subject, "what you plan on doing after you've retired. Have you got family around these parts? Going traveling, or just going to spend more time fishing?"

Ben Wainright shook his head wearily. "No, I'm tired. I think I'll just go back to where I came from." He looked Mitch in the eyes. "I've been waiting for you for a long time. Thank you for coming in, Mitch."

"Oh okay." Mitch shrugged. "My pleasure."

That didn't make much sense, he thought. He only just got the job. He guessed Wainright was waiting on someone, anyone, to take over.

The old doctor steered him toward the door. "I'll finish up now."

"Guess I'll see you at the mayor's this weekend," Mitch said brightly.

"Enjoy the practice." Wainright ushered him out and headed back into his office, leaving Mitch and Shelly alone.

"Where he came from?" He turned to Shelly. "He's been here all his life, and he's going home? To where?"

She shrugged. "I've worked with him for two years, and he keeps a lot to himself. Most do around these parts. We mind our own business. It's what we Eldoners do."

Mitch nodded, and then turned. "Hey, did you ever hear of the Angel Mine, or Angel Syndrome?"

Her lips pursed for a moment. "Nope."

"Okay, forget it." He gave her a little salute. "Nice to meet you, Shelly, and see you soon."

CHAPTER 04

Mitch headed out and down the front path, still thinking about the Angel Mine. He'd read a few historical reports and also some old newspaper clippings that stated many people died in the turn-of-the-last-century underground collapse, with some ensuing site contamination.

It was the one mystery about the place that intrigued him. Especially as there was further information about some weird affliction in the seventies—Angel Syndrome—that Wainright undoubtedly experienced first-hand as he was working here at the time it broke out.

Odd that Wainright blew it off as being just a few minor skin irritations. Maybe when he got hold of the practice, he could do some more digging; he was sure some of the other old-timers around town might remember something.

Mitch's boarding house was on the outskirts of town and from what he could remember, it wasn't all that far from the actual mine site—maybe just 20 minutes driving on an empty road. This time of day? A piece of cake.

It was still only just gone 3:00 in the afternoon; he could probably take a quick run out there and then still be home in time for dinner.

"Just do it."

Mitch jumped in his car, checked his maps, and then pulled out and kept going straight until he came to the main road. Then he turned right, heading back along the highway. Mitch sailed down the wide road, passing only a few trucks and SUVs, but as he expected, it was as quiet as a holiday weekend.

He didn't really know why he had an interest in the mine; curiosity maybe. *Angel Syndrome*. He thought about the term. As a medical man, his interest was piqued. And the filing cabinet in Wainright's office was one of the few repositories of information he knew of, yet the old doc wanted to destroy it.

Something was a little off there, he thought.

Mitch slowed at a rusted gate. He checked his maps once again and guessed this might have been the turnoff. There were no signs, and nothing to indicate this once had been one of the largest and most prosperous limestone mines in America.

That was then, he thought. After all, it was more than half a century ago, and not exactly a tourist hotspot. He got out and went to open the metal gate. It wasn't locked and even the hinges had rusted through so it was just propped upright. He simply lifted and laid it out of the way.

He drove up the track and after another five minutes or so came to a stand of stunted trees around an open patch of ground. There were a few abandoned railway carts, or jerry carts he believed they were called, plus a stack of spare rails rusting away in the afternoon sunshine.

He got out of his car and the first thing that assailed him was the acrid, dry smell of chalk and limestone. But there was nothing else; no birdcalls or the background *zumm* of crickets and cicadas. It seemed that it wasn't just the people that had abandoned the mine.

Mitch was about to head off when he stopped and returned to the car to rummage in the map compartment, then the middle box, and finally the door slots.

"*Damnit.*"

The flashlight wasn't there, and for the life of him he couldn't even remember removing it.

"Just when you need it." He sighed as he straightened. "Lucky I have the night vision of a cat." He chuckled, hitched his pants, and walked toward the mine mouth.

Old, rusted cyclone fencing was strewn around, and he carefully stepped over it. As Mitch headed closer to the large opening, he noticed there were a few scabby and gnarled trees that had long surrendered to the lifeless, dry dirt. There were also strange and twisted columns of stone about, and just like the trees, these were also contorted into weird shapes.

He stopped closer to one and stared. Mitch narrowed his eyes, not able to tear his eyes away from the odd thing. *Perhaps it wasn't stone after all, but petrified wood*, he wondered, as it looked like ancient tree bark. And if you looked at it from just the right angle, it could have once had facial features carved into it.

He crossed to another of the petrified pillars and peered in even closer. The features and detail were beginning to weather away, but whoever had done the work had been quite skilled. The sculptor also had an eye for the macabre, as the face looked to have a mouth hanging open as if wailing, and in torment.

"Creepy as fuck," he whispered and finally turned away to head to the mine mouth.

Mitch saw that the cavernous mine mouth opened into a three-foot-deep shallow basin in the earth with one end a dark hole sunk into the ground, leading down at a gentle slope. He eased down into the recess and walked toward the opening.

"Damn." It was blacker than the darkest night inside that hole. He squinted, waiting for his eyes to adjust, but it made no difference, as only a few dozen feet in, there was simply not enough light even for a shadow. No human eye would ever adjust to that.

"Not even enough light for a cat," he said softly.

He sniffed deeply. Even though it had been dry for weeks in these parts, he detected an odor of dampness from the yawning pit. Mitch decided to breathe slowly in and out through his nose—though he bet any water had long receded down to the depths of the mine, he was still wary of the contamination Wainright had mentioned. And he certainly didn't like the idea of starting work covered in some sort of weird rash either.

He didn't know how long he stood there staring into the stygian darkness, but he knew it would be useless to go in without a light. Useless and dangerous.

People died down there, and he couldn't remember reading whether their bodies were ever recovered. If not, then in effect it was a mass grave.

"*Hello-ooo!*" he shouted.

The echo bounced away into the dark tunnel and repeated several times until silence finally returned.

He grunted and was about to turn away, when he thought he heard what sounded like a small dragging noise from down deep in the caverns.

He spun back.

He waited, concentrating so hard he felt his unblinking eyes begin to burn. His hand went to his hip, reaching for his gun that wasn't there anymore, but old habits never died.

What big predators lived in these parts? he wondered. Were there cougars, bears? He continued to stare, frozen to the spot; there was something moving in there, he was sure of it.

He'd done night-time incursions before, but then they had night vision goggles, and he'd been armed and armored up to the teeth. Now he had nothing but his wits.

"*Hel…*"

Mitch was about to call again but suddenly realized he didn't feel like making any noise, and certainly not venturing any deeper into the mineshaft. He didn't like the odds.

I'll come back with a light, he thought as he backed up a few steps, keeping his eyes on the impenetrable darkness of the mine mouth.

As he made his way back to the car, he saw a knocked down sign: "*WARNING – No swimming, no bathing, no drinking. Ground water contaminated. By order of the Eldon city council, Oct. 1978.*"

Mitch exhaled; it was a year after the outbreak. He turned back one last time to let his eyes run over the mining grounds. He changed his mind—he didn't think he would come back with a light. In fact, he didn't think he'd want to come back at all.

CHAPTER 05

Ben Wainright had watched the young doctor depart from his window. He was so young, so full of confidence and energy. He had been like that once.

He sat down slowly in his chair and felt the weight of the aged flesh settle on his bones and the heavy burden of guilt on his conscience.

He sat there staring down at his desk, seeing nothing as his mind took him back again to Eldon in 1977. Back to the very first case.

*****

"I'm sure it's just the flu, Mary. It's the start of the season after all." A young Doctor Benjamin 'Ben' Wainright smiled reassuringly at the woman who hung on his every word as if he had just climbed down from the mountain with a stone tablet under each arm.

He knew that in a small town the local doctor's opinion mattered and was only one step below that of the Lord. Therefore, his job was to soothe nerves as well as heal wounds.

Mary Hepworth was widowed and struggled to look after her ten-year-old son, who now sat silently, staring straight ahead. The boy had presented with symptoms that he'd been seeing quite a lot lately—listlessness, sleepless nights, loss of appetite, and unlike a fever-heat, the kids had the opposite in that their core temperature was on the low side.

The only worrying symptom he couldn't account for was a roughening of the skin on the back, thighs, and hands. Right now, those tiny hands grasped the armrests of the chair and to the naked eye only looked a little darker than his normal skin tone.

"Aspirin, orange juice, and early to bed." Wainright smiled as the woman nodded and helped her son to his feet.

Wainright turned to a large jar that held plastic-wrapped lollypops and lifted out a red one and green one.

"Billy, which one?" He held them out.

The boy didn't even turn.

"Billy?" He moved them in front of the boy's face.

The boy's hand lifted slightly but then hung in mid-air for a moment before he wrinkled his nose and shook his head. He dropped his hand and turned away.

"*Hmm.*" Wainright kept the reassuring smile on his face, even though a kid refusing candy was a huge red flag. "When was the last time he had a good meal?"

Mary seemed to search her mind for a moment. "Yesterday. No, the day before when he had a cookie, but that's all."

"Okay, you've got to try and get some food into him. He needs his energy to fight this bug, and a cookie is not going to do it." He looked down at the kid. "Will you help your mom out there, Billy?"

Billy nodded dreamily.

"Good boy." He tussled the boy's hair and felt a few tiny, hard lumps on his scalp, but put it down to the kid also needing a good bath. Wainright then shook Mary's hand. "And call me in a day or so to let me know how he's getting on."

"Yes, Doctor." Mary guided the boy to the door, and he opened it to let them out.

Wainright caught sight of his waiting room and was surprised to see it full of anxious-looking parents with their children, and a few adults by themselves. *Whatever it is, it is going around*, he thought. He closed the door and quickly jotted down some notes.

The days rolled on, and then the weeks. The first flurry of parents bringing in their children dwindled and then stopped. He wanted to believe that the bug or whatever it was had burned itself out. But the thing was, he hadn't seen a single one of the people who presented with the original symptoms.

Zero follow-up was too good to be true, and then his receptionist, Margie, told him that the local schools were only half full—those kids were probably still at home.

Still.

Curiosity and a local doctor's desire to care for his community overwhelmed him.

"If the mountain will not come to Doctor Wainright…" he got to his feet and packed his leather doctor's satchel, "…then Doctor Wainright must go to the mountain."

Ben climbed into his sky-blue Plymouth Duster and groaned, immediately wishing he had parked in the shade. He quickly wound down the window to release some of the furnace-like air from the interior. He would have done the same on the opposite window but couldn't be bothered reaching across.

One day, they'll have machines to do that for us, he mused. He pulled out and enjoyed the breeze chilling the perspiration on the back of his neck.

It was a short drive to the Hepworth place. Though the tarred road ended a while back, the dry weather of late meant the dirt road was solid—rutted, but solid.

On his way, he passed a single figure, a Native American, with long, dark hair shining like a raven's wing in the sunshine and held back by a cloth headband. He slowed and the man turned toward him. Wainright didn't recognize him from town and guessed he must have been just passing through.

Wainright slowed; the young man must have been no more than mid-twenties, with a blanket roll over one shoulder and a cloth satchel bag under his arm. The pair of men stared at each other for a while until Wainright felt he couldn't meet the youth's gaze anymore as it seemed to burn right into his soul and pluck the thoughts straight from his head.

Wainright accelerated away and in the rear-view mirror saw the man still staring after his car. *Strange*, he thought and made a mental note to mention it to the sheriff.

Only another mile down the road, he pulled up out front of a small, well-kept home and tapped the horn twice.

Ben Wainright got out and stretched his back, feeling the wet shirt unglue from his body. He was a tall man and regarded as being quite dashing. He'd come unannounced so he waited a moment in the sunshine, expecting Mary to appear on the front deck and forgive him for his unexpected intrusion.

After another moment, still no one had appeared, so he walked briskly up the front steps, twisted the bell twice, and heard it ring loudly inside the house.

He gave it another minute and then peered in through the glass panel and saw Mary coming slowly down the hallway. She wiped her hands on a cloth and tucked it into the waistline of her skirt before opening the door.

The pretty young mother looked drained of color, and her eyes were red-rimmed from either lack of sleep or crying. Ben guessed both.

"Ben." She made his name sound like a lament.

"Mary?" He stared for a moment. "Ah, I came to check on Billy. Is everything okay?"

After a moment, she shook her head, and her voice was little more than a squeak. "Not really."

"May I come in?" He stepped closer.

"*Um…*" Her head was down and she wrung her hands for a moment, but eventually she nodded and shuffled aside.

Ben stepped inside the doorway and pointed to a closed door from memory. "Second on the right?"

She nodded again and he proceeded down the hallway to Billy's room. But Mary stayed put.

"Follow me, please," he said over his shoulder.

As he neared the door, he slowed and reached out a hand. But for some reason, there was a tingling in his stomach that hinted at a strange nervousness that shouldn't be there. He shook it away, twisted the knob, and pushed the door inward.

The first thing that hit him was the smell—fish, rotting vegetation, methane, and excrement. He'd never actually smelled what a fish shit out of its body, but he bet it smelled like this.

"He had an accident," Mary whispered.

It was dark inside, and he reached for the light.

"Don't," she said, voice quivering.

He paused with his hand hanging in the air and half-turned. "I need to see what I'm doing. I'm sorry." He flicked the light on.

The scream that came from the mess of soiled bedcovers made the hair on his neck rise—it was an animalistic screech of pain and torment, hardly had any human notes in it at all. It continued to fill the small room.

"*Billy*," Wainright yelled forcefully.

The boy immediately quietened but had burrowed down below the covers. Wainright glanced around the small room. On the bedside table were numerous plates, many still piled with spoiling food. A few looked to have been at least nibbled at, but just the meat he noticed.

There was also a bedpan tucked under the bed that had a few tiny logs of dry feces piled inside. *It probably doesn't help the smell in the bedroom*, he thought. He nudged it to the side so he could approach the bed and then sat on its edge.

He looked up at Mary. "I'm going to examine him now, is that okay?"

She just stared, not at him, but at the rumpled mound of blankets.

"I'll take that as a yes." Wainright reached out. "Billy." He laid a hand on the mound. "Billy." He felt the hardness below and was surprised by the sharpness of some of the edges on his body. Rather than a ten-year-old boy under the covers, it felt like someone had thrown a blanket over a tree stump.

"I'm going to have to pull the covers back now, Billy."

The mound shook violently for a few seconds, so he paused.

"Does the light hurt your eyes?" he asked.

There came something like a nod from the top end of the mound.

Wainright sighed, determined to press on. "I need to examine you, so just keep your eyes shut."

The mound jiggled violently again, and there came a sound like a hoarse exhalation that devolved into a sibilant hiss.

Wainright had had enough. "Sorry, Billy, I'm just here to help." He yanked the blankets back.

He sucked in a breath and leaped to his feet. The boy was naked, but from his head to his groin the skin was totally grown over by some sort of hardened growth. From his back, there extended things like branches, but that spread wide, giving the impression of wings.

The boy looked up at him with a face that was as horrifying as it was pitiful. Small, yellow eyes glared, and the mouth opened, showing a rim of needle-like teeth that seemed to ring the entire mouth and would have been more at home on some deep-sea predatory fish.

Billy mewled and placed hands over his face that were

encrusted claws. Wainright swallowed in a dry throat and steeled himself as he carefully sat back down. He lifted a hand and reached out to place it on the boy, but froze—*infection*, his mind screamed.

Wainright drew his hand back, stood up again, and leaned forward. He licked his lips. "Ah, Billy, tell me where it hurts."

There came a soft mewling again and then a rasping sound. Wainright leaned closer. "I didn't catch that, Billy."

"*Allllooverrr.*"

"All over?" Wainright repeated. "It hurts *all over* your body?"

"*Yesssss.*"

Wainright felt a growing knot of anger in his stomach. He straightened and turned to Mary. "How long has he been like this?"

She shook her head for a moment, and he noticed her eyes were wet as she stared at her son. "Days."

Wainright scowled. "He's been in this condition for days? How could you…?"

"He wouldn't let me." The words came in a rush and her eyes slid away from her boy's to his. "It just began as a coarse rash. But it got worse, then this started growing all over him." She clasped her hands together as if begging him. "He wouldn't let me tell anyone. Made me promise."

"I'll need a sample." Wainright reached into his bag for some gloves to pull on and also found a disposable hypodermic needle. He gently laid a hand on the boy's upper arm and felt the strange texture beneath his fingertips. It didn't feel like skin at all and more like exposed bone or maybe even something akin to tree bark.

He'd read about afflictions that resulted in a thickening and hardening of the skin's epidermal layer. But this seemed beyond anything he had ever seen or heard of before.

"Just stay still for a moment, Billy." He pressed the needle into the arm, but the point wouldn't penetrate the skin. "Damn." He drew it back, looking at the tip. He'd have to find an area that wasn't so calcified.

Wainright looked back at the boy who had pulled the blankets back over himself. He went to peel them back again.

"I haven't quite finish…" The boy suddenly lunged at him.

Wainright pulled his hand out of the way just as the needle-sharp teeth came together in the air where his fingers had just been.

"My God." He leaped to his feet, staring.

The boy pulled back beneath the blankets and kept his small yellow eyes fixed on Wainright. The doctor felt his heart thumping in his chest. The kid looked like some sort of vicious animal retreating into its burrow. He swallowed noisily.

"I'll, *ah*, need to do some analysis, Mary. I have no idea what it could be right at this moment. I'll consult the medical texts when I get back, and also make a few calls.

"I still need…" He quickly crouched to grab Billy's bedpan, "…this."

Billy grumbled as he retreated fully into his nest of blankets, and Wainright looked briefly into the bedpan at the small, speckled logs—it certainly didn't look like a human bowel movement. He was confused and a little frightened.

"Mary, do you know if he ate anything, or came into contact with anything strange?"

She seemed to search her mind for a moment, and then looked up. "The mine. All the kids go and swim at the mine, as it's the first time it's been flooded in years. Billy said when the water dried on him it made him a little itchy."

Wainright knew the place; the Angel Mine was just outside of town, and though home to a disaster way back early in the century and all closed up now, sometimes the ground water percolated to the surface and created an oasis. It was rare, but it would be irresistible to kids on a hot day, he bet.

"Okay." He started for the door and once outside pulled it shut. He lowered his voice. "We'll need to send him to the hospital. Get professional care from experts and some decent food into him. We can't have him lying here like this all day."

"But he doesn't," she whispered. "He goes out at night."

"Goes out? Like that?" His head pulled back on his neck. "How, where?"

She looked up at him, moon-eyed, and slowly shook her head. "I don't know where. But I hear the window open about midnight."

He waited but she just went back to wringing her hands.

"Okay. *Ah…*" He held the bedpan and looked around. "Do you have…?"

"Yes, yes." She bustled away.

Wainright looked down at the boy's bowel movements again. They were dry, oval, and had white flecks through them. He'd seen coyote scat before, and it reminded him of that.

He was hoping for some sort of container or bag but Mary came back with just a cloth that she draped over the pan. It wasn't sealed but he didn't think it'd make a mess as long as he kept it upright.

She then led him to the door and stood to one side, watching him. With his medical bag in one hand and the bedpan in the other, he could only nod and give her his most reassuring smile. "Don't worry, Mary, we'll sort this out."

She nodded. "Please…"

He paused.

"Please help us," she whispered.

*****

Ben Wainright sat back from his desk for a moment and pondered his next move. There were other children affected, lots of them, and it now seemed to be some sort of outbreak of…*what?* He had no idea, but after examining Billy's excrement, he found it contained nothing but digested protein, fur, and animal bones. It seemed the boy's night-time foraging was where he was getting most of his sustenance.

His old filing cabinet was now near full of cases, and he knew it was time to admit defeat. He pulled out the small, black leather-bound address book he had in his top drawer that all physicians kept. It contained emergency numbers for everything from fires and flooding, to nuclear bomb fallout. It also had the number for the Communicable Disease Center—termed the CDC—that had been around since the mid-40s, and he had never thought he'd ever have to call in his life.

He circled the number and lifted the phone. This was out of his hands now.

*****

Ben Wainright was there when the vans arrived—dozens of them, all black. He felt like some sort of informer, handing over a list he had drawn up that identified the families, where they were, and then assisted in allying those same family's fears when they were rounded up for detailed medical treatment at a facility in the big city.

Some of the children were in the early stages of the affliction, with just mild skin rashes and fevers. Others were like Billy and had onset deformities with the bony protrusions all over the bodies. But then again, some were barely recognizable as children anymore, and even had branch-like growths from their backs that resembled wings—*Eldon Angels*, he heard one of the CDC guys mutter. But it was far from angelic, and rather more frightening and revolting—*and not just for the parents*, Wainright had thought.

If they were angels, they were fallen ones, he muttered.

He'd watched as most went willingly, some fearfully, but all hoping for answers, a cure, or perhaps just an end to the horrifying ailment that was plaguing their children.

Not all the kids were found, as some were assumed to have gone feral and simply melted away into the countryside. Or worse, the rumor was that they disappeared into the depths of the Angel Mine.

Long after the vans had gone, Wainright headed out to the mine and saw that a line of new cyclone fencing and multiple warning signs had been erected. He'd heard that the water hole that the flooded mine had created had drained away again, perhaps back to its subterranean lake where it originally came from.

He stood in the sunshine for some time, feeling the heat of the noonday sun sting his neck. He imagined the whoops of delight from kids leaping into the water—boys and girls, freckle-faced, sunburned cheeks and bronzed shoulders.

They were all gone now, contaminated, and those found were herded away in the night—all on his say-so. He felt sick in the heart as he turned back to the path leading to his car.

"*Adotte Sakima*."

The sudden voice nearly made him jump out of his skin. Right there in front of him was the young Native American man he had seen on the road.

Ben Wainright held up his hands. "I don't want any trouble."

"Who does?" The youth shrugged, and then faced the impenetrable darkness of the mine mouth. "The curse is not gone, you know?" He turned back to Wainright. "It only waits."

Wainright backed down the hill. "I'll keep that in mind."

"Good, remember it. Remember everything that happened here." The Native American picked up his satchel. "Because I can't hold it forever."

"Okay. Got it. Thank you." Wainright turned away and scrambled down the loose rock of the rutted path to his car. He pulled open the door and jumped into its furnace-like interior, slammed the door, and quickly ducked down to look through the windscreen back up the hill.

The young man was gone. "Crazy." Wainright swallowed hard onto a hammering heart.

He started his car and turned in a tight circle, shooting loose rock out behind him. He'd had enough of curses, people turning to wood, and *Adotte Sakima*, or whatever the guy had said. Right now, he was going home to get good and drunk.

CHAPTER 06

Eldon, Missouri – today

Saturday morning and Doctor Mitch Taylor sat at a window seat in the coffee shop and sipped from a mug of coffee the size of a soup bowl. Everything seemed bigger and better out here, and much better value.

He had time on his hands and had decided to wander into town. His first weekend and he was excited, as everything was new and interesting, and he'd loved exploring ever since he was a kid.

He looked up and down the main street, deciding on his exploration plan—first, he'd go up one side of the street and come back down the other, doing a bit of window shopping, and maybe introduce himself to a few of the shopkeepers.

He saw that down opposite the council chambers was the Eldon Museum, and it certainly wouldn't hurt to bone up a little more on his newly adopted home's history.

Mitch finished his coffee and then walked up the street to the plain, white-painted building with the glass double doors and cupped hands to each side of his face to peer inside. It had just gone 10 am, and though there was no "*Sorry, we're closed*" sign hanging on the Museum door, he didn't know if they even opened on Saturdays.

There was a flick of movement inside so he dropped his hands, grabbed the large brass doorknob, and turned it. The door opened smoothly, and he pushed into a smell of chalky mustiness and dry air-conditioning.

"Hallo-*ooo*." The musical greeting made him smile and a woman bustled toward him with hands clasped in front of her.

She pointed. "It *is* you." She beamed. "You're our new doctor."

Mitch raised his eyebrows. "My notoriety precedes me."

She laughed softly. "You had a write-up in the Eldon Gazette just a week back. You look just like your picture." She held out a hand. "It's nice to meet you, Doctor Taylor."

"Nice to meet you too and please call me Mitch, Ms…?" He returned the smile.

"Alston, Samantha Alston, but call me Sam. And thank you. I'll call you Mitch out here, and Doctor when I'm visiting. Okay?" She raised a pair of tiny eyebrows.

"Works for me." Mitch grinned back.

She leaned a little closer. "I'm also president of the ladies bridge players club."

He nodded, knowing he was meant to be impressed. "Nice."

"So, you've come to take in some of our history?" she asked.

"Sure have."

"Then let me take you on a personal tour." She rubbed her hands together and turned. "Follow me."

The museum wasn't large; maybe in the past it had been a converted, larger type house of one floor that now had been partitioned into open display rooms for each of the period themes.

She pointed at certain relics, pictures, or artifacts, and gave him a brief overview of each. She was pleasant, knowledgeable, and quite entertaining. Mitch was enjoying himself.

She paced as she kept up her stream of information about when Missouri was first settled, the state's oldest town, founded by French Canadian colonists in 1735.

Then she stopped and gave a tiny shrug. "But our little town of Eldon never made an appearance until 1882 and is a relative newcomer to the landscape. It's said that it was the old stories that apparently stopped a lot of people from settling out here." Samantha turned.

"Stories?" Mitch asked.

"Yes," she declared, but then, "well, maybe *legends* is a better word. In those days, superstitions and belief made a huge difference to what people did and didn't do."

"What sort of legends?" Mitch asked, intrigued.

"Well, though Eldon is a young town, and Missouri is only just on 400 years old, its history is far, far older." She half-turned. "Well beyond our history."

She led him into the back of the museum and switched on some lights. "There were seven ancient tribes in the area of what is now called Missouri: The Chickasaw tribe, the Illini, Ioway, Missouria, the Osage, Otoe, and the Quapaw tribe."

She stopped before a large case that held what looked like several statues. "And these are some of the mysteries of the area. The history of the Black River area of Missouri goes back to the Paleo-Indians, the ancient peoples of the Americas who were present at the end of the last ice age. They camped and hunted along the Ozark River, perhaps as long as 14,000 years ago."

"Wow, that *is* old." Mitch blew air between his lips. "I never knew." He craned forward. "And they made these?"

His brows came together as he looked at a group of strange-looking statues upon a raised dais.

"We believe so, but we don't exactly know how. Or even where the unique material came from." She briefly turned to him. "It's petrified wood, but from no tree anyone can identify." She peered in at the statues. "It's been dated to around 10,000 BC—that's 12,000 years old."

Mitch stared. The statues were intertwined with roots and slightly eroded now, but the detail was still unbelievable. There were several men, women, and even a child. Their fingers and even hair could be picked out. But it was their faces that were the aspect that pinned Mitch's attention—they wore ghastly expressions of pain or terror. Or perhaps torment.

He recognized them. "You know, I think I've seen something like these before. Down near the old Angel Mine, there looked to be very weather-beaten versions of these out front at the mine's mouth."

She tilted her head. "Why would you go there?"

"*Um*, well…" He gave her a lopsided grin. "I don't know; I was just exploring, I guess."

"I don't think it's safe. My mother…" She stopped. "I've never been out there…and never will," she added. "Might be similar, but I doubt it. Probably just some weird geology that had been sand-blasted, or an old tree stump fashioned by some of our harsh summer gusts."

"Yeah, maybe." Mitch looked back at the agonized faces. "Not exactly uplifting images."

"No, not at all. And the conundrum is that the first American Native Indians who lived around these parts led a Stone Age lifestyle, meaning they only had stone tools and weapons. So, it's still a mystery how they even worked the stone-like material, or what they were meant to represent with their, um, *extreme* visages. The one thing all the local tribes had in common was the name of a powerful god: *Adotte Sakima*—the tree god."

"*Adotte Sakima*." He tested the words as he continued to stare, and the more he did the more unsettled he became by the statues. They were tiny perfections that were beyond anything he'd seen before, especially from an artist that created them so many millennia ago.

One of the men had a slightly balding pate, the woman had an adornment through her earlobe and a small lump like a mole on her lip, and the child's tiny hand was curled as if it was holding something that might have once been a toy.

Mitch hadn't seen that level of sculpting complexity even on statues from the ancient Romans, and perhaps only from sculpting masters like Michelangelo.

But the horrifying expressions? He didn't get it. "What could generate such fear?" he breathed out.

"Men only fear God and the Devil," she replied softly.

"Maybe the tree god was their devil, *huh*?" He glanced at her and then back to the statues. "When and where were they discovered?"

"Just after the town was settled," Samantha replied. "They were found deep below the ground in some limestone caverns. We can only assume the first people must have taken them down there."

"Why?" he asked.

She shrugged. "No one really knows. But there was one man, a Native American, from the Otoe people—Johnson Nightbird—who was the closest thing we had to an expert and helped us set up the display."

Mitch straightened. "I'd love to talk to him. Is he still around?"

She bobbed her head. "I don't even know if he's still alive, as he must be 80 by now. If he is, he'd be over in Red Rock, Oklahoma."

Mitch nodded. "Might have to look him up one day." He checked his watch. And then smiled broadly. "Thank you, Samantha, you've been very informative and entertaining; I think I've learned a lot."

His eyes flicked back to the statues.

"See you at the cookout," she chimed.

He pulled his eyes away. "Hope so." He headed out the door, glad for the fresh air and sunshine.

Without a doubt, those things unsettled him more than they should have. They say soldiers have an intuition and an inbuilt radar for danger—and for some reason, his radar was flashing right now.

CHAPTER 07

The send-off for Old Ben Wainright was an afternoon cookout at Mayor Keith Melnick's large house just on the outskirts of town. Mitch was looking forward to the formal goodbye for Ben, but really, his main interest was talking to Karen again—there was something about the spunky vice mayor that turned his head.

He stepped out of the shower, toweled himself down, and then used his fingers to brush his hair. He stood just looking at his reflection for several moments and thought he still looked passable.

He worked out and was in good shape but had a few flaws now. He reached up to his chest and shoulder to feel some of the most obvious shrapnel wounds; purple circles and strokes, and some surrounded with reddish flesh where the damage went deep and that still ached when he did bench press. As a physician, he knew what that meant; he'd pay for it when he was older. But that was something he'd worry about another day.

In another 30 minutes, he was pulling into the driveway of Melnick's large house set on a huge expanse of very manicured lawn. Fruit trees lined the fence line, creating a never-ending bounty that glowed red, orange, and purple in the warm sunshine.

There was a good crowd already, and fronting up he spotted the town attorney, Ralph Gillespie, talking to Karen who stood beside a boy that looked remarkably like her, so it was safe to assume it was her son.

Mayor Melnick spotted him and waved. Though he felt like a bit of a small fish among the town heavyweights, he guessed as he was their soon-to-be doctor, he'd end up knowing all their secrets soon enough.

"Mitchell, glad you could make it." Melnick toasted him with an iced cool-looking, highball-style drink and grabbed his arm. "Got some people for you to meet. Settling in? Found everything you need? How do you like Eldon so far?"

Mitch grinned, knowing all the questions probably weren't expected to be answered. Just the obvious ones.

"I love it here. I'd say it's just like home, except this is better."

Melnick was extremely satisfied with his answer and grabbed his forearm, steering him toward a group of older people. At the same time, he motioned for a waiter to bring him a drink.

"They're mai tais." He winked. "My own recipe. Got a bit of a kick to them." His laugh was a soft wheeze.

Karen caught his eye and he waved. She made a show of waving back and nodding, and she obviously used it as an excuse to extricate herself from Gillespie and headed toward his group, dragging her son with her.

Ralph Gillespie tagged along behind, but the look he gave Mitch said he didn't care for the intrusion.

"Mitch, meet Benji. Benji, meet Mitch," Karen said, looking from her son to Mitch. "Mitch is our new doctor."

Benji stuck out a small hand and grinned. "Pleased to meet you, sir."

Mitch gripped the small hand. "Likewise. And it's just Mitch to my friends."

The boy smiled and continued to study him for a few more moments before half-turning to his mother.

"He looks like Batman, doesn't he, Mom?"

Mitch chuckled at Karen, who now also scrutinized him. Mitch knew what Benji was referring to. Just like Gladys had mentioned, many times in the past people had said he reminded them of a young Ben Affleck…except with a few scars. He could certainly live with that.

He leaned closer to Benji and put a finger to his lips. "That's because I'm Batman. Just don't tell anyone, okay?"

"Great, we have a doctor who's a superhero." Karen grinned.

Mitch chuckled. "All doctors are superheroes—it's lesson one at med school."

He took another sip of his mai tai and grimaced. "*Yech*." He stuck his tongue out, much to Benji's amusement.

Karen laughed. "The secret Melnick recipe, *huh*?"

"Oh yeah." Mitch toasted her. "And should have stayed secret."

Mitch was enjoying himself and found Karen to be interesting and charming. He hoped she felt the same. But after another 30 minutes went by, Mayor Melnick moved in among them.

"Okay, Mitch, what have you done with him?" Melnick smiled good-naturedly, but it was clear that this entire expensive event was for Ben Wainright, so the guest of honor better front up. And because Mitch was the guy taking over the practice, Old Ben had somehow become his responsibility.

"Anyone called him yet?" Mitch asked.

"I'll do it now." Melnick pulled out a paper-thin phone and examined his contacts before letting it dial. He waited, and then his brows drew together. "That's odd." He pulled the phone away from his ear and looked at it. "It says the number is no longer in service—was canceled days ago." He frowned. "He's still in town, right?"

"Sure is, I just met with him yesterday morning," Mitch replied. "I haven't seen him since then, but he didn't say he was leaving. Well, not immediately."

Shelly, his receptionist barged in, having overheard. "He should be here. He's usually very punctual."

"Well, even if you've left town, you don't cancel your mobile phone." Ralph Gillespie had joined, and a small crowd was now gathering.

"He should be here." Shelly folded her arms.

"Do you think he's all right?" Karen asked.

Mitch felt in his pocket. "I've still got his spare house keys. I can take a quick run out there."

"I'll come," Shelly piped up. "Maybe he just has car troubles, and now that his phone isn't working, he can't tell us."

"That must be it," Melnick agreed. "Mitch, go get him."

"On it." Mitch walked fast to his car, and though the party continued, it had formed into clumps only talking softly, and right up until he was driving away, their eyes were on him.

In the car, Mitch cracked the window to let in some fresh air and relief from the clouds of Shelly's perfume. He half-turned. "Had Ben, Doctor Wainright, been feeling okay before he retired? Acting normally?"

She hiked her shoulders. "He didn't talk that much to me in the office. But he was always polite, just a little sad, distant sort of." She seemed to think a little more. "He was always quiet, except for the time we had the fire."

"Fire? In the office?" Mitch's brows shot up.

"Yeah, a few years back. Just after I started. The sandwich toaster overheated." She grinned sheepishly. "And it was next to a stack of papers, files."

"And they caught fire." Mitch tilted his head and raised an eyebrow. "Shelly, was it *your* sandwich toaster?"

She nodded slowly. "Yeah, Ben made me do a lot of extra photocopying work of his records after that. Took me weeks."

"And does Doctor Wainright have a no toaster rule now?" Mitch asked.

"Yep, plus no coffee machine, or even juicer." Shelly's mouth was pressed in a line.

"Okay, I think we'll keep that rule for now." Mitch grinned and concentrated on the road.

They came off Newton Street and turned into Mills Street. He slowed the car.

"There it is, number 2. That's Doctor Wainwright's place." Shelly craned forward. "Ooh, and he's burning rubbish at this time of year—very naughty."

They pulled in at the column of smoke. It was a well-kept cottage with a slatted fence, vines growing through it, and a rusted post box just peeking over the top. They sat watching the rising smoke for a few seconds.

"Would he have forgotten about the party?" Mitch asked.

"No. He's old, but not out with the squirrels old, if you know what I mean," she replied.

Mitch was first out of the car, and he immediately smelled the chemical stink of plastic burning.

"I don't think he's burning leaves. Or even squirrels. Come on." He walked briskly up the path and then bounded up the few steps to the landing. He pressed the bell.

"Just open it." Shelly came up quickly behind him.

Mitch half-turned. "Just give him a second." He waited.

Shelly cupped her hands around her face and peered in through a window. "Nothing moving inside." She came back and stood on the other side of the doorframe. "Come on, he might have fallen down. He's old, remember?"

"Yeah, okay." Mitch sorted through the keys, choosing one that looked like a front door key. He stuck it in the lock, and it turned first go. He pushed the door open and peered around inside.

"Hello? Ben?"

Mitch concentrated but heard nothing but the deep and ponderous ticking of a large clock somewhere further in.

"*Doctor Wainright.*" Shelly's voice flooded the cottage, but after a few more seconds there was still nothing but the clock again. "Come on," she said and led Mitch in.

She quickly went from the living room to his bedroom, opened a closet door and found it empty. Same for the drawers, as all the clothing and personal items were gone.

"Strange. Looks like he's all packed up," she said and turned slowly. "Try the kitchen and washroom." Shelly was obviously speaking to herself, as she sped out of the bedroom.

Mitch tried to keep up. "Slow down."

The house looked like it had been vacated and even the refrigerator was empty.

"What's he been living on?" Shelly pursed her lips and then slowly let the refrigerator door close. She then quickly crossed to the window over the sink and peered out into the backyard.

"There's his bonfire and also the only place left to look—the shed." She pulled open the backdoor, stepped down the few steps, and marched across the 50 feet of grass to the small wooden structure.

Mitch followed and saw that the rubbish pile was still smoldering and giving off toxic chemical gasses. Then he saw the reason—within it were the remains of jackets, pants, and even leather shoes. There was also a laptop computer, something that could have been a blackened mobile phone, and piles and piles of papers, books, and melting plastic folders.

Just at its edge was another set of keys. Mitch crossed to the smoldering pile and carefully reached in to grab them.

"Ouch." The carbon-encrusted keys were still hot, and he tossed them from hand to hand for a few seconds.

"Hurry up," Shelly hissed over her shoulder.

"Something is very wrong here," Mitch said as he caught

up.

She grabbed the large door handle and turned to him. "Maybe he already left." She tugged open the paint-peeling door that skidded along the ground. Now wider, it allowed the single room to be flooded with light.

Shelly gasped, eyes bulging. Mitch looked in over her shoulder, and even though he had seen horrific things as a military medic, this took him by surprise.

Ben Wainright was hanging by the neck; face black and tongue protruding like a fat, dark slug from between his lips. A small stool was overturned below him and also a small pool of fluid, undoubtedly urine.

"Stay there." He rushed inside to grab the body. Immediately, he felt the cold, stiffness of rigor mortis in the cadaver and he let it go for a moment where it now swung, making the rope stretch and squeak.

Shelly hadn't moved but finally managed to close her mouth. "He…hung himself? Why did he hang himself?"

Mitch righted the stool and was about to step up, but then thought that it was a good question. Though the probability was he *did* commit suicide, in the event it was something else, he should avoid disturbing the body.

He backed up, bumping into Shelly. "I don't know, but we better not touch anything else. Let's call the sheriff." Mitch grabbed her arm and led her out of the shed, but she kept looking back over her shoulder as if expecting Wainright to jump out at them.

Mitch dragged the door shut and sighed. He knew he'd need to make calls to the sheriff, to the mayor, Karen, and all this while they're back at the party sipping on Melnick's mai tais and waiting for their guest of honor, who was now rudely swinging from a damn noose.

In 30 minutes more, Sheriff Dan Kehoe was on his way, and the mayor was breaking it to the party that their beloved Doctor Ben Wainright wouldn't be making it for cake, ever.

"Shelly, as the resident medical professional that has to act as both physician and coroner, I have to hang out here for a while. But you don't. Do you want me to drop you somewhere? I doubt the party will be continuing now."

She looked back toward the house and slowly shook her

head. "I want to know why he killed himself." She folded her arms. "I'll wait…with you."

It was barely ten minutes more before Sheriff Kehoe arrived. He was alone and as he got out of his car, his face was grave.

"Show me," was all he said.

CHAPTER 08

Eldon, Oakland County, Missouri – 2 weeks later

The ground began to shake.

Mitch had just come into the practice and was standing in front of Shelly's desk when it hit. He stopped to hold his arms wide a little like a tightrope walker.

"*Whoa.*" He looked up, arms out, newspaper in one hand and coffee in the other. "What was that?"

She smiled and shrugged. "Probably a little quake. We get 'em now and then. I heard they come from down deep and are due to some big old caverns collapsing, and not when the planes or plates or something moves. Nothing really to worry about."

"Tectonic plates," Mitch added. "And you mean the mines?"

She wrinkled her nose and shook her head. "No, I think I remember it was more like the big sinkhole type ones wa-*aaay* deeper down. Eldon sits on ground that's a little like honeycomb. The deep limestone melts away, leaving big holes."

Mitch raised his eyebrows. "Good for spelunking."

"For what?" She grinned. "Spunking?"

"*Spel-LUN-king*—caving," he said on his way to the office.

"Oh, that." Her mouth turned down. "I'd hate that 'cause I hate dark places."

"Yeah, not really on my bucket list either." He lifted his chin. "Appointments?"

"Yep," she said, beginning to read from the schedule on her screen. "Mrs. Abernathy at 9, John Jamison at 9:30, and Mrs. Oswald is bringing in her son at 11."

"Good." He meant it. He needed work as a distraction following Ben's suicide.

As coroner, he'd checked Ben Wainright over and it was straightforward strangulation. Jumping from a stool doesn't break the neck, so death doesn't come quickly; instead, it's just a slow choking.

Without his hands tied behind his back, it takes real willpower to go through with it. Ben must have really been determined to check out.

He paused. "Hey, how you doing? About Ben, I mean."

She bobbed her head from side to side for a moment. "A bit bummed. But okay. And you?"

"Yeah, yeah, just…confused more than anything else."

Shelly's eyes bulged and she pointed past him to the open window. "*Rat*!"

"*Huh*?" Mitch cringed from her shriek and spun to see a large black rat moving along the windowsill to then drop into the garden.

"That thing was huge."

She snorted. "Yeah, and been here for years. I call him Willard."

"Well, it's not a good look for health professionals to have a pet rat on the premises. So, Willard goes." He looked at her from under lowered brows. "Can you organize…?"

She sighed long and loud. "Yes, I'll get someone to catch him."

"Thank you." Mitch headed into his practice rooms. He recalled that after finding Ben when he had first returned to the practice, he'd found a stack of letters in his desk drawer addressed to many of them—himself, the mayor, Karen, Ralph, and most of the other councillors and town elders. They all contained just two words: *forgive me*.

Forgive him for what? His suicide? Maybe. Or was there something else? Some other *thing* he had been carrying around in his head that generated some industrial-grade guilt that had finally overwhelmed him?

Mitch remembered something and turned in his chair to look at the large antique and formidable wooden filing cabinet in the corner. He sat staring at it for several moments. It was the only thing he hadn't got around to investigating.

He crossed to it and ran his hand over the exterior—oak probably and he bet it weighed 200 pounds and maybe another 100 fully loaded. He pushed it a little and it didn't budge even a fraction.

He pulled at the top drawer and that also didn't shift. "Yep."

He stuck his finger in one of the brass keyholes in the drawer face. He knew it'd take a large, old-style Mortise-type key with the rounded barrel. And he'd just found one.

Mitch went back to his desk and opened the top drawer in his desk where the heat tarnished set of keys still sat. He snatched them up and knew before he even tried it that it was going to be the right one.

What secrets was Ben trying to hide? Were they what he was shamed by and sorry for? Mitch went back to the filing cabinet. *It is time to find out.*

He stuck the key in and turned it. The lock moved slowly but went all the way around—*success*. He tugged the top drawer open, and it came out way too easy.

"*Shit*."

Inside was empty. And the next drawer, and then the last one. He suddenly knew what else was in old Ben's bonfire.

"Taken to the grave." He tossed the keys up onto the cabinet top. "Thanks, Ben."

CHAPTER 09

Red Rock Canyon Creek, Oklahoma

Johnson Nightbird stood on his front porch, hands in his old denim jeans pockets, and looked up at the sky. His once raven wing-black hair was now silver and still hung past his shoulders, but his eyes retained their sharp hawk-like gaze.

He knew it was coming again and also knew he needed some spiritual fortitude before he was called upon to engage the ancient adversary.

It was time. He sighed, stepped off the porch, and walked the track through the forest toward a secret area beside the canyon creek where the water slowed in a belly and where no one ever came.

He easily found the cave even though heavily overgrown and he pushed in past the thick brush to stand in its mouth for a moment. It was known to very few surviving members of the Otoe tribe and he inhaled the cool air that emanated from deep inside. He hadn't been here for 50 years, but it had left a scar on his spirit that was still as raw as if it were carved there just yesterday.

There were torches ready and a tin of lighter fluid that he squirted on the rag tied at one end. He flicked his small lighter to life and held the flame to the soaked cloth for a moment to ensure it took, then he drew in a deep breath and headed in.

The cave narrowed for 100 feet or so then opened out into a larger cavern, and Nightbird stood at its center and turned slowly. On the walls were ancient images drawn all around him in a mosaic that was laid down by the first people. They were those beyond the ancestors of his own tribe—stories going back over 14,000 years.

The old Native American knelt, held his hands in front of him palm up, and then began to chant loudly, his voice sing-song and echoing in the darkness. He let his eyes run across the images painted on the walls that told of a story that had begun so long ago, it was old even as the first people recorded it.

There were the bound warriors who were being led into the cave and then a descent into the deep darkness, to a fate worse than death. There were horrors that waited deep-down and all held dominion over by the ancient one—the *Adotte Sakima.*

He didn't want to go back there but knew he would soon be called. He let his chant fall away and shut his eyes.

Johnson Nightbird was aware his physical strength was ebbing with age but in here, he felt the spirits of the ancestors draw close to him, whisper to him, and fill him with light and strength.

He lifted his head. "One more time," he muttered and rose to his feet.

CHAPTER 10

Eldon Sparkling Mineral Water Company, Eldon

"Boss, Well 24 has just gone dry. And 25, 26, and 27 are running dirty so we shut 'em all down." The engineer looked up from his clipboard. "The quake, most like."

The tiny Shih Tzu under the desk was going bananas, barking like a mad thing at the intrusion.

"Shit-damn. Knew it." Harry Reith was owner and president of the company, and there was one thing he hated about working in an area riddled with limestone—it damn moved, and when it did, it sometimes swallowed their water.

He turned to the dog. "Shut up, Pompom." The other thing he hated was when he had to look after his wife's damn fart-puff of a dog while she went into town.

He sighed. The quakes opened seams or vents and their water sources could drain away, be cut off, or silted up for years and rendered unusable as it clogged the pumping machines. Though they did significant testing to ensure no contaminants got into the water, like heavy metals, silicates, or composite toxins, the upside of their wells being so deep and so old was there was little chance of water-borne bugs in it.

"What about the new well? Site 30?" Reith asked.

The engineer scoffed quietly. "Funny thing that. When the geologists first identified site 30, it looked to only have a few hundred megaliters of water. But after that little shimmy we just had, they tell me that it now stands at several gigaliters—it's now more like a damn underground sea."

"Looks like that's where all our water went." Reith shrugged. "So, tap it."

The engineer tilted his head. "Might be a little dirty."

"You already tested it, right?" Reith asked.

"Yeah, when we first found it, but…"

"You know what we sell other than water?" Reith half-smiled and didn't wait for his engineer to respond. "That's right, nothing. So, pump it up, scrub it, filter it, and let's go. We got orders to fill."

The engineers snapped the note board shut. "On it, Chief."

CHAPTER 11

Benji Powell's pushbike was raising dust as he only just kept pace with his pals. The day was hot, and the four boys and two girls pedaled like demons.

Out front were James and Kenny, followed by Isabella, then him, and at his shoulder was Gemma, and finally lagging behind was big Alf, puffing hard as his stomach bounced as he navigated the small bumps and pits in the old roadway.

It was a brutally hot day, and the small group headed out to the old limestone mine, as there had been stories that had intrigued them following the quake. If true, their summers were about to get a whole lot more fun.

"Here." James swerved off the road and onto the disused track. The kids all skidded, pedaled on, and stood in their seats to pick up their pace again.

It took another 20 minutes to get to the first fence whose lock had long since corroded away. They headed in, carefully threading their way around old machinery, disused railings, and rusting jerry carts.

They'd all been out here many times in the past, but back then it was dry as chalk dust and just as uninteresting. There had been a few gnarled stumps of weird-looking rock trees and dust covering everything. They'd tried to venture into the mine once, but after only a few dozen feet they gave up, as the darkness had creeped the shit out of them.

Back then, they'd settled for throwing rocks into the old mine mouth and listening as they bounced away into the impenetrable darkness. But this time, when the small group arrived at their destination and stopped in a line, their mouths dropped open. And then slowly curved up into grins.

"It's like one of those places in the desert…you know," Alf wheezed.

"Yeah, an oasis." Benji let his eyes move slowly over the

landscape.

The once dry and scrabbly ground out front of the mouth of the mine was set in a shallow depression a few hundred feet across and just two to three deep. It had been dry, cough-inducing, and boring. But not anymore.

Now the depression in the ground was filled with a huge pool of sparkling water. It had a slight greenish tinge, but in the hot sunshine it was so inviting, it screamed at you to *come on in*.

The quake had only happened a few days ago, but amazingly, the surrounding plants had already improved. The twisted trees didn't have leaves, but their bark was ribbed, glossy and fuller, and more, *muscular* looking. There were also patches of thick grass that had sprung up and even small fern fronds touched on the edge of the water.

Benji smiled and softly repeated the word: "Oasis." And that's exactly what it was.

James got off his bike and let it fall with a clatter. He started to pull off his shirt. "I'm in there."

"Wait, what?" Isabella pointed to the rusting sign with barely legible writing. "You saw that contamination sign, right?"

"No, yeah, whatever. That was 100 years ago or sumthin'." He pointed. "Besides, look at the birds."

Benji and Isabella turned. There were several birds perched on the edge of the pond dipping their beaks into the greenish water and then tipping their heads back.

"If it's okay for them, then it's okay for us. Nature knows best, right?" James' narrow chest was now bared to the sunshine and he began to undo his jeans. "C'mon everyone… *c'mon*."

James, Kenny, Gemma, and Alf walked carefully across the scrabble until they made it to a grass verge. Benji shook his head as he saw Big Alf's jelly belly bounce as he walked to the water's edge. The only things he wore were his tighty-whities, and around his neck a bottle cap-sized silver Saint Christopher medal his dad gave him when he was about five.

Kenny was already in and surfaced spitting a stream of water from his mouth. He spat again. "Tastes weird." He grinned. "But feels great. *Come on*!"

James turned back to where Isabella and Benji still sat

astride their bikes.

"Chickens." He tucked his fists under his arms and flapped stunted wings for a second or two before turning back to the magnificent water, finding a deeper spot, and leaping in.

CHAPTER 12

Harry Reith was down in the Eldon Spring Water testing facilities and didn't like that his scientists looked concerned. And if they looked concerned, then he was concerned.

"Looks a little…green." He held Pompom under one arm and in the other hand he held the glass of water up to eyeball it for a moment before sniffing the top. "And there's an odor. What is it?" He looked to Pete Coughlin, his lead production manager, from under lowered brows.

Coughlin took the glass from him. "Zero bacterial count, normal mineral count, and been run through various filters leaving nothing toxic behind." He sniffed the glass as well. "It just seems to be some sort of plant residue. Might be organic and might not be, but probably safe though."

Reith exhaled through his nose and raised an eyebrow at his technician. "Let me be frank; it stinks like shit. I wouldn't drink it." He looked up. "And this is from the new well, site 30, right?"

"Yep. I'm thinking the tremor stirred it up a little." Coughlin shrugged.

"A little? It's fucking soup," Reith scoffed. "Doesn't look like mountain spring water to me and more like something you'd get from draining a fish farm."

"We could put it through micron filters or use evaporation methodology to take out any of the residual microscopics, but that's time-consuming and expensive. It'll cost you more than what you can sell the water for. From a commercial perspective, for now, I'm pretty sure that's as good as it gets." Coughlin stuck both hands in his coat pockets.

"*Shee-it.*" Reith exhaled through clenched teeth. Looks like he had three choices: overpriced clean water, dirty water, or no water. He sighed. "We'll need to find another goddamn well. We'll miss our delivery dates."

Coughlin began to grin.

Reith scowled. "Okay, smartass, what?"

"Well, I was just thinking that seeing as we're pretty sure it's safe to drink, so for all we know the unknown residue might be good for you." He shrugged. "It's just a little stain and a little smell. So what? We can mask the odor with a few drops of lemon flavoring. Then we sell it as a mineral health drink."

Reith's brows unknitted and slowly began to rise. "But no artificial stuff, right? Pure health tonic."

Coughlin nodded. "Of course. We use citral—comes straight from lemon oil extracted from the peel. Natural as your granny used to make."

Reith rubbed his chin for several seconds and let his vision turn inward for a moment. "And you're sure it's safe?"

"I'm betting as safe as any of our products. And as safe as our testing can assure us." Coughlin lifted his chin, looking confident.

Reith thought about the implications, and then the opportunities. He spun back. "Brilliant. Make it happen." He headed for the door. "I'll be up in marketing getting the guys to knock up some labeling." He turned as he got to the exit. "If this sells, I'll give you a bonus that'll put a smile on your face bigger than Texas."

"Thank you, sir." Coughlin gave a small bow and then turned to clap his hands. "All right, people, we've got some work to do."

PART 2 – THE ANGELS RETURN

CHAPTER 13

Eldon, the Adams' residence

"I've got a headache…and a sore throat." 10-year-old Kenny Hatfield grimaced as he demonstrated swallowing for his mom.

Andrea lifted the small flashlight again. "Say *ahh*." He did so and she peered in. "It's very red in there." She gently laid a hand on his forehead.

He winced. "Ow."

She pulled her hand away. "That hurts?"

He nodded and swallowed again. This time, she actually heard it make a dry clicking sound in his throat.

Her brows knitted together. "Does your head hurt on the inside or outside?"

"Both."

She shone the light in his eyes, and he screwed them shut. His forehead hadn't felt hot to the touch, but she did see some odd bumps and marks appearing like the beginning of a pebbly rash. "Okay, no school tomorrow."

"*Yes*." He settled back into his soft pillow.

Andrea paused at the door. "But that doesn't mean a day playing computer games. You'll do extra homework, okay?"

"*Aww*." Kenny rolled away. "Might as well go to school." He briefly rolled back. "Only kidding, I'm sick."

Andrea's lips curled into a smile. *A day off school cures everything*, she thought.

*****

Hours later and Kenny Hatfield still couldn't sleep. His head throbbed like there was a big ole hammer beating in it; plus, he had the worst taste in his mouth. He reached up to trail his fingers over the top of his sore head.

"Lumpy," he said softly as he felt the knobby things over his skull and dropping his hand, he saw his fingers come away covered in hair. He didn't know what it meant, but it scared him a little.

"*Mom*!" he yelled.

Shouting made his head throb even more. He raked his hand over his head again and drew an even bigger clump of hair.

"Mo-*oooooom*….!"

The door opened and his mother came straight in and flicked on the bedside lamp. The sudden burst of light was like a dagger into both eyes that penetrated his brain.

He screwed his eyes shut tight, expecting them to water, but there seemed no fluid in them at all. Keeping his eyes closed, he just held up his hand.

"What happened to your hair?" Andrea reached forward to grab his head and run her hands over it. "Does it hurt?"

"Just my eyes. Turn the lamp off, please," he asked.

She did and then hugged him. "Get dressed and I'll take you down to see the new doctor."

"No," he said quickly. "Just tired now."

She seemed to think for a moment. "Well then, we'll see him first thing, okay?"

"'Kay." He nodded, distracted. "Goodnight."

She kissed him and went out but left the door to his room ajar. Kenny lay in bed facing his window. He could hear something, he was sure of it—a calling or singing, and it was the most beautiful thing he had ever heard in his life. It took away the pain in his head and replaced it with…magic.

He drifted off and smiled at the things it whispered to him, that it told him to do, and what it said he could become.

He knew then that everything was going to be fine.

CHAPTER 14

"Creepy kid," Shelly said out of the side of her mouth.

Mitch glanced at her. "Don't talk about our patients like that. Especially when they're feeling unwell."

She raised her eyebrows. "Gloves, hoodie up over his head, and dark sunglasses at ten years old? And screaming when the light got in his eyes. Yeah, unwell is an understatement. What was up with him?"

"*Shelly*," he warned.

"Oh, come on." She smiled. "I have to type up his records anyway, so you might as well tell me now."

He sighed, knowing she was right. "Young Kenny Hatfield, nothing serious, just some sort of flu-like virus, I presume. Rash, dry mouth, sensitivity to light. Bed rest for a few days, plus I've given him a shot of B12, and some general antibiotics for now."

She nodded. "Don't forget the holy water."

He glared at her and she held up her hands. "Okay, okay, last time I crossed the line I had to do about 50 years' worth of photocopying in a month."

He chuckled. "That's what happens when you set fire to a doctor's surgery. We have 100 ways to make you suffer."

She scoffed and grinned back at him.

Mitch suddenly had a thought and turned to her. "Hey, what copying?"

She waved an arm around. "Everything, all of it. All of Doctor Wainwright's files. He didn't trust them being all at the surgery anymore."

"*All* of them?" He stood.

"Yeah." She frowned. "He must have told you." She winced. "Oh…sorry."

"Did you happen to copy the contents of the old cabinet? The antique wooden one in his office?" His eyes gleamed.

She nodded. "I think so."

He crossed to her. "Where are they all now? Are they cataloged?"

"The library storage facilities. And yes, I'm very good at filing," she replied.

"Then I have a job for you. Right now," he said quickly.

She groaned.

"I want you to go to the library storage facility and retrieve the box or boxes of copied material just from the old antique filing cabinet. Can you do that, please?" he beseeched.

She shrugged. "Sure, no problem."

*****

Mitch sat staring at the pile of brown, nondescript folders on his desk. None of them were labeled with names or places, but instead there were simply dates and sometimes numbers.

But inside were notes, and pages and pages of the small, tight writing style of Doctor Ben Wainwright. Some had Polaroid photographs, and all mostly dated from early 1977.

Many were headed: *Angel Mine Syndrome* with a case number, and Mitch tried to get his head around the story they told, especially considering the man had told him to his face that there were only a few minor instances of infection and skin irritation.

But the reality was, back in 1977 there was some sort of horrifying outbreak that primarily afflicted the children. Over 20 boys and girls fell ill to a condition that drove gross deformities in the skin, muscle, and skeletal structures and also seemed to affect their thinking, making them exhibit psychotic behavior. At first, he thought the children were incongruously labeled: *angel children,* or just, *angels.*

Until later.

The first case was of Billy Allison who didn't live that far from where Mitch lived now. His mother Mary had brought him in with a rash on his lower back. In a few days, it had progressed to significant crusty extrusions that coated most of his body and much of his face.

There was a shadowed and grainy color Polaroid that showed a small figure in bed. Mitch squinted and was sure the eyes were yellow—not like jaundice yellow, but almost a glowing, nocturnal stare.

"*Jee-zuz,*" he whispered.

Some of the other pictures of different children were impossible to comprehend maybe because of the poor camera equipment used. But as far as Mitch could make out, many didn't look like children anymore at all, but instead some sort of creatures assembled from bony plates and tree bark. He grimaced at the next images—and some were worse.

Now he understood where the "angel" term had come from. A few of the kids had things growing from their backs that resembled branch-like structures but spread wide like wings. Mitch blew air between his pressed lips.

"Holy Hell," he whispered.

There was nothing Mitch knew of anytime or anywhere that could do that to people. Even severe mutagens that scrambled DNA and cell structure acted slowly, and usually ended with the body simply corrupting with cancerous cells, not looking like it was trying to remake itself…into something else.

Wainright had been understandably overwhelmed and had called in the authorities. The CDC arrived first, and then some other government types that Wainright noted he never found out who they really were.

The children, all of them that could be located, had been evacuated, and from what Mitch read and understood from the notes, none of them ever returned. Not them, or their families.

Where did they go? Mitch wondered.

Wainright blamed himself for informing on them, but what else was he supposed to do? He had no chance of curing or even diagnosing what was happening to them.

Mitch had so many questions, but the only person who could have answered them had just taken his life.

He felt sorry for old Ben Wainright, keeping this to himself all these years. He just gave thanks he'd never be tested like the old man was.

Mitch paused at the thought. He'd just seen young Kenny Hatficld with a skin rash.

Not the same thing, he thought confidently. But then… He might just check in on the kid tomorrow.

CHAPTER 15

Marshal Simmons wiped his hands on a rag and jammed it into the back pocket of his blue coveralls. The sun was down now, the last of his mechanics had gone home, and he was getting ready to shut up shop.

There were a few vehicles waiting for some minor work, but only a few. Business was getting tough. The new cars these days were basically computers on wheels. They hardly ever broke down, and you didn't put your head under the hood to see what was going wrong—you simply plugged them into some other computer thing and let it run a *diag-nos-tic* over the entire system, from its air-conditioning to the transmission. Then the damn thing told *you* what work it needed.

He sighed. There wasn't enough in the kitty to afford one of those things, and so for now, he relied on the old-timers like himself to bring in their aging autos.

Marshal didn't have any kids to leave the garage to, so when he retired or died, the garage would die with him. *That's progress*, he thought glumly.

The smash of glass from the rear of his workshop snapped his head around.

"Who's there?" He stared into the darkness.

The sound wasn't repeated, but a sixth sense told him he wasn't alone anymore. Marshal walked softly to a workbench and grabbed up a long, silver wrench and then tiptoed between two cars toward the dark rear of the shop. He immediately regretted not flicking the overhead lights back on, but that'd mean backtracking now.

There came a skittering sound, and he wondered whether there were raccoons in the building. If one of his mechanics had been leaving food in the bins, he'd skin 'em alive.

"Garn, *git*!" he yelled.

The workshop remained silent.

Marshal had two options: he could flick on the lights and spend hours doing a search of the workshop for some critter making mischief in here. Or he could leave it until tomorrow morning when the sun was up.

Easy decision.

"See you tomorrow." He tossed the wrench onto a bench top and turned away.

The thing that landed on his back was damn heavy, and hard, and no damn raccoon. It felt like it was made of rock or wood as its fingers or claws dug into the meat of his neck while hissing like a boiling kettle.

"Get offa me!" he yelled while waving his hands over his head.

His flailing left hand got bit, crunching the bone and making blood spurt. Marshal was forced to the ground and wailed as the thing then started to drag him, its claws digging deep into his flesh like daggers.

He skidded across the floor and managed to catch sight of himself in the glass doors—it didn't help; the thing that had hold of him was basically human-shaped, but shorter, and it moved weirdly like an insect, with skin that was all horny and rough.

"*Help*!" he yelled.

And it was enormously powerful as it dragged him as if he weighed nothing. It leaped up onto a bench and went straight out through a broken window, taking Marshal with it.

"*He-eeelp*!" he yelled again. But no one came, no one heard.

My garage is dead now, he thought as he was quickly drawn away into the dark woods.

CHAPTER 16

Harry Reith held up the bottle of mineral water. The label showed the Eldon Spring Water brand and also had the words "*super health tonic*" in green calligraphy blazed across images of a crystal-clear lake, waterfall, and trees filled with rainbow-colored birds. The bottle's glass was also green to hide the pale green tinge of the liquid, but as they had called it a health tonic, it didn't really matter.

"Looks good." He turned to nod to the assembled marketing, sales, and technical teams. "I'd buy it."

He twisted the top and heard the hiss of escaping gas. He sniffed and then shrugged. "This is where the rubber hits the road." He lifted it to his lips and sipped. He smacked his lips for a moment and then sipped again, longer this time.

He lowered the bottle and grinned. "This is good. Just a hint of lemon that combines with whatever shit was in there to give it quite a unique flavor." He chugged down some more. "We might be onto a winner here."

Reith took a few steps toward the window that looked out over the car park as his mind worked. Branding and advertising got people to buy their first bottle. But it was up to the flavor factor to bring them back for the next one.

He spun back. "Okay, let's go with it, high scale. I want full production, ten thousand units per day to start. We'll do a sample population test right here in Eldon, and if it works, we'll move it out nationally to all our regular big buyers."

Pete Coughlin grinned from ear to ear. "You got it, boss."

"And get to work on some slick ads we can run nationwide. This could be the next big thing. And we don't even need to add caffeine or sugar—it'll be the healthiest drink on the market."

He tipped the bottle up and drained it. "This is damned good. Well done, everyone." He headed for the door but paused. "I want it in everyone's icebox by week's end."

*****

Just before dawn, the morning deliveries were being made to the many cafes, restaurants, convenience, and corner stores in Eldon. In among their usual deliveries of milk, soda, and alcoholic drinks was a crate of brilliant green bottles.

On the side of the crate were the words "Eldon Spring Water – Super Health Tonic." The samples were free, and before noon all had been given out to the public or at least tasted and approved by the shop owners…

Who all made follow-up orders—the new spring water was a hit.

*****

Harlen Bimford carried the crate into his shop and placed it into his cool room. He pulled out several bottles, stuffed way too many under one arm, and carried them out. When the heavy door closed behind him, he held one up to examine it. He liked the color and the labeling.

He nodded his approval. "Real interesting."

He'd place several in the glass-fronted ice box and also one on the counter as a display—you know, for sales purposes. After all, as the ole saying goes: *eye level is buy level*. He chuckled.

As he carried the bottle, Buford, his old hound got under his feet. Harlen tripped and one of the bottles hit the ground, popping its lid so half its contents spilled over the floor.

"Dang it, Boo. Go on, get out now."

The dog's ears drooped, and it got belly-low to the ground. It looked up at him with one of those crushed expressions only a dog could conjure.

"Aw, I'm sorry, boy, you're okay."

Buford immediately recovered his sappy dog grin and wagging tail. Harlen placed the remaining bottles on the counter and snatched up the now half-empty one from the floor. He took a sip.

"*Ahh*, that is good." He wiped his mouth. "Oh well, guess I get to sample the stock after all."

He turned to see Buford lapping up the puddle, and he laughed softly.

"You never need a mop when you got a dog." He sipped again from the green-tinged bottle.

CHAPTER 17

"Alfie? You up there, son?" Hank Bell waited at the bottom of the attic steps, staring up into the dark void.

Alfie was Big Alf to his friends, even though he was still only ten years old and to his dad would always be little Alfie, the kid with the chubby face, toe head, and cheeky grin.

The kid was a bit of a scatterbrain but friendly and lovable, and that was why it was odd that he had been spending too many days up in the attic by himself for it to be normal.

Come to think of it, Hank hadn't even seen the cat for a few days either. Probably no real problem. After all, Patches might just be up there keeping him company; one thing about felines was they loved the dark mystery of a basement or attic.

Hank had thought nothing of it when early on Alfie had moved some bedding stuff up there, and he thought he was just making some sort of fort for him and his friends to hang out in. But then he hadn't caught up with Benjie, Kenny, Gemma, James, or any of his usual posse for ages.

"I'm coming up, okay?" Hank grabbed the railing and began to haul his bulk up the steep steps. He puffed after just a few; too many beers and not enough exercise had slowed him down, and he knew it.

His head came above the attic floor and he hung there for a moment. It was gloomy, and his eyes found it hard to adjust to the darkness. And he could see that the globe overhead had been removed.

Why would the kid do that? he wondered. Weren't they supposed to be afraid of the dark—Hank swallowed—like he was now.

Dummy, he thought. He should have brought a flashlight. He contemplated going back down to get one when a small mewling noise brought his head back around.

"Patches, that you, kitty?" He came up a few more steps.

"Alfie?"

He licked lips that had suddenly gone dry and noticed the weird smell. It was bad, and he wondered if the kid was relieving himself instead of using the toilet. He'd catch hell if he was.

Hank started to come up a few more steps and placed a hand on the attic floor but jerked his hand away. His fingers came away sticky and he saw something dark on them. He held them to his nose, sniffed, and his brows came together.

Phew, he thought. Bad, but at least it wasn't shit. He wiped his hand on his pants.

"Alfie, where you at, boy?" He stepped up into the attic and cast around for the removed globe to at least give himself some more light.

There was an object the size of a baseball and also scraps of something covering the floor, and he bent lower waiting for his eyes to adjust a little more. He pulled back, baring his teeth in revulsion—the mounds were scraps of black and white fur, and the thing he thought was a ball was their damn cat's head.

From out of the darkness, the thing leaped onto his back. Hank fell under its weight and immediately things like needles fixed to his upper shoulder near his neck.

Rage, and fear for his son, filled him. If whatever this thing was had killed the cat, maybe it had also attacked his son.

He rolled over, fighting. Whatever it was, it was hard and made a furious animal sound as it ripped and tore at his flesh.

Hank managed to throw it off and the thing thumped brittlely on the floor then skittered away into the darkness.

He flipped over and scrabbled to his feet. "Alfie, *where are you?*"

His instincts were to flee, but he lumbered further into the dark, knowing his son was the priority.

Hank felt the warm wetness spill down his side, and his hands stung from the sharp spikes or thorns on the thing. Anger fueled him, and he'd either find his son or stomp the animal that attacked him until it was nothing but a busted shell.

Something dropped on him from the ceiling beams and he felt talons piercing his flesh. It hissed like a snake and clung to him, stabbing at his body, piercing his flesh in dozens of places from the thorns or spikes again.

Hank went down on his back this time and clung to the thing even as it shredded his skin.

In the light from the open door to the downstairs, something glinted that was hanging around the horror's neck. Through blood-filled eyes, Hank could make out what it was, and his world came crashing down.

It was a Saint Christopher medal.

Hank then knew where Alfie was. He dropped his hands, surrendering because he didn't want to fight it anymore.

CHAPTER 18

The days rolled on and soon became weeks. Things were quiet in Eldon—no more tremors, no more kids coming in sick, and the Hatfield boy, Kenny, that he had treated as well as his family, had suddenly moved away.

The only thing that changed was a new soda appeared in a few iceboxes, but otherwise, there was nothing but peace, sunshine, and smiles.

Mitch had treated Karen for an ingrown toenail, and though he was busting to ask her out on a date, he knew that it wasn't good form to ask out patients, especially while treating them.

Luckily, he didn't have to because Karen asked him over for a quiet family dinner with her and Benji.

He whistled as he put his tie on. He had no idea of whether he would be overdressed or not, but if he was, he guessed he could always take it off.

He continued knotting, unknotting, adjusting, and then reknotting his tie as he listened to the radio. The local news was informing them that the search was continuing for the missing families. It seemed that small groups of people were vanishing or leaving, and oddly, not telling anyone they were going. Not even relatives.

Hmm, just like Kenny Hatfield's family, he thought.

The next report was on the livestock attacks in the outer areas of town, and given there were grey wolves in Missouri, they were high on the suspect list.

Well, at least things were quiet in town, he mused.

Mitch checked himself one last time in the mirror—still looking good, though a little tired around the eyes. Maybe he'd look better if Karen's lighting was a little dim. He had a bottle of red wine ready which he snatched up as he headed for the door.

She was over on the other side of town, but given Eldon

central only covered a few square miles, he'd still be there in no time.

Saturday evening, it was warm and dry, and the streets had a few people wandering to the cafes, restaurants, and probably the only cinema in town. Turning off the main strip, he wended his way to the northern outskirts and quickly found Karen's neat little two-story cottage.

He pulled up out front and saw that her Jacarandas were in bloom. The South American trees had lilac flowers that when they began to fall created a carpet of crushed magenta in her garden. In through the window, he could see the golden glow of candles making the interior look warm and inviting.

As he stepped out, Mitch sucked in a deep breath, feeling the tingle of butterflies going mad in his belly.

Come on, buddy, you're 35, not 15, he thought as he straightened his tie, suddenly feeling constricted, which made his face hot.

He walked up the steps, stood outside for a moment to compose himself, and then reached toward the bell just as the door was pulled inward.

Benji was grinning up at him, his hair slicked down, and his probably bestest ever clothes on. He turned and in his most ear-splitting outside voice yelled, "Mo-*ooom*, Batman is here." He turned, grinning even wider.

"*Coming.*" Karen's voice floated down from upstairs.

Mitch waited. "Is there a password?" he asked.

Benji nodded.

"Gotham." Mitch lifted an eyebrow.

Benji looked serious for a moment as he seemed to think about it. "Yep, that was it." He stood aside.

Mitch stepped inside and the boy shut the door. "This way."

He led Mitch into their living room that was lit with candles, and he looked up at Mitch and rolled his eyes.

"We have lights and don't always use candles. But for some reason, Mom wanted to do it tonight. Do you like candles?"

"I do. Reminds me of a birthday party," Mitch observed.

Benji looked around, nodding. "Yeah, it does sorta." He turned back. "She spent all day cleaning."

Mitch chuckled. "Best leave some secrets."

He looked up at Mitch, surprised. "It's not a secret." He

waved an arm around. "See, look how clean it is."

"*Hallooo*." Karen breezed in wearing a tight cotton dress, hair immaculate, and all finished with a pair of old sandshoes.

"You look magnificent," he said, meaning it as his heart leaped in his chest.

She lifted a foot. "The ultimate in sensible shoes."

"On you, they look good." He chuckled. "And the toe?"

"Much better." She dropped her foot. "But I desperately wanted to wear nice shoes and got as far as trying some on—painfully bad move."

He nodded. "Give it another few days."

"That's the plan." She spotted his wine and held out her hand. "For us?"

He handed it over. "Yeah, it's red, is that okay?"

She looked at the label. "Yes, and very nice." She turned. "Benji, grab us the two wine glasses from the table."

He scampered off and came back with two enormous glasses. She took one, and Mitch the other, and then she opened the wine and poured them both a good splash. She held out her glass. "Thank you for coming."

He clinked her glass. "My absolute pleasure."

She pointed at the couch. "Sit down while I finish up in the kitchen. Benji, keep our guest entertained." She vanished down the hallway still holding the wine bottle and glass.

Mitch sat, sipped, and put his glass down. He saw the boy sipping something red as well.

"What's your poison, buddy?"

Benji grinned and held it up. "Blackcurrant juice. Mom doesn't let me drink soda, as she says this has more vitamin C and doesn't make your teeth fall out." He hiked slim shoulders. "It's okay."

"It certainly is." Mitch made small talk with Benji about school, his friends, favorite holidays, and anything else he could think of. In turn, Benji wanted to know about the grossest things he had ever seen as a doctor.

In another moment, the aroma of chicken filled the air and Karen called them to the table.

"I warn you, cooking is not my forte," she said with a crooked smile.

He looked at the table and the huge pot in the center, still bubbling with something red and hearty inside. Small, crusty rolls were on each of their plates and the silverware was laid out.

"Chicken and bacon pasta, with spinach and tomatoes."

Mitch inhaled; it smelled as good as it looked. "Fantastic." Mitch inhaled again, feeling his stomach rumble.

"Is it your favorite?" Mitch turned to Benji.

"I don't know, I've never had it before." Benji's eyes traveled over the pot. "Smells real good though."

Karen laughed softly. "Yeah, okay, cats out of the bag—we're road testing a new recipe tonight."

The meal proved as good as it looked, and Mitch was delighted to only end up with a few spots of tomato on his tie. Dessert was hazelnut chocolate pie and ice cream, which was even more to Benji's liking.

In between mouthfuls, he kept up his conversation. "Mom, Mitch was telling me about the grossest things he's seen as a doctor."

"Probably not great dinner table conversation," Karen replied.

Benji was undaunted. "Tell her about the old man with the giant wart on his nose." He looked from Mitch to Karen, his eyes wide. "It was as *big* as his nose. And when it was cut off…"

Karen sighed. "Gross, *stop*, no thank you."

"Comes with the territory, I guess," Mitch said. "At least it wasn't as bad as the stuff that came out of the Angel mine."

Benji frowned. "What?"

Mitch nodded. "Finally got to read old Ben Wainright's notes. About 50 years ago, seems there was some sort of contamination outbreak that came from kids swimming in the flooded mine."

"They got sick?" Benji's eyes were wide.

"Yeah, real sick," Mitch said. "Not good. He kept the details in a locked filing cabinet and burned them. But luckily, we found copies. It was really horrible."

"Just from *swimming* in it?" Benji's voice had risen.

"Doctor Wainright thought they were swimming in or drinking it." The boy looked pale and Mitch started to regret bringing it up.

Karen stared for a moment. "I never knew. I guess it's a good thing that it's dry now. And has been for decades," she added.

Benji slowly put his dessert spoon down and stared straight ahead.

CHAPTER 19

The next morning, Mitch arrived at Hank Ball's place at five past eight after receiving a call from the mayor himself. He'd been told to bring his medical bag—not a good sign.

As well as the mayor's car, he also noticed Sheriff Kehoe's cruiser pulled up out front—an even worse sign.

He looked up at the two-story house; it needed a bit of work with peeling paint, some wood rot in the windowsills, cracked roof tiles, and way too many leaves in the gutters.

He'd met Hank and his son Alfie, and they were nice people, and as Hank's wife had passed away a few years back, the big guy was managing to raise his son on his own and doing a faultless job.

The front door was open, and Mitch stood just inside. "Hello?"

"That you, Mitch?"

"Yo." Mitch headed in toward the sound of the voice.

Along the front hallway, he came to a set of steep steps leading up to the attic with both the sheriff and mayor standing at the bottom, waiting.

Kehoe nodded. "Doc."

Keith Melnick's normal, gregarious good humor was missing from his expression. Mitch also noticed that the sheriff held a large and powerful flashlight like the ones you usually take camping.

"Thank you for coming out, Mitch." The mayor exhaled. "Need your professional opinion on something." He turned. "Sheriff."

Kehoe started up the steps, followed by Mitch and then the mayor. It was dark in the void above the house and Kehoe turned on the light before they reached the top of the stairs.

"Bulb was out; I replaced it," he said over his shoulder. "And I mean removed, on purpose."

As soon as Mitch arrived up in the warmer air of the attic, he smelled the blood and offal—he recognized it immediately, as he'd been on enough battlefields to know the odor of death when he smelled it.

"Over here," Kehoe said.

Mitch's shoes made a tacky sound on the sticky floor and Kehoe lifted his light to a mound of ragged clothing in the corner. As they approached, Mitch saw it was more than just clothing with the protruding ribs, pelvic girdle, and the tufts of blood-matted hair that were still attached to a lacerated skull.

"That's Hank. Or was," Kehoe said. He pointed his light beam at an object a little further in. "And that was their cat."

Mitch glanced at the tiny, separated head and flaps of drying skin with fur attached, and then back to the ruined corpse of Hank.

"What happened?" Mitch asked.

"You tell us," Kehoe said, sounding like he was breathing just through his mouth. "Got a call from the school wondering where the kid was, so I came out to their property. Didn't find him." He nodded toward Hank. "Found this instead."

Mitch crouched. "Jesus, what a mess." He looked up. "When?"

"About an hour ago, give or take."

Mitch nodded and turned back to the corpse. He reached into his bag, pulled out a pair of disposable gloves, and put them on. Then he gently took hold of the exposed ribcage.

"Little more light here."

Kehoe obliged.

Mitch saw then that the internal organs were all gone, which was fairly indicative of a large carnivore —take the soft, high blood-filled organs like the liver, lungs, and kidneys, and then chow down on the heart muscle.

Mitch had seen bad shit before, but poor Hank's face was hard to look at; it had been obliterated, as the nose and lips were gone, with both the eyes punctured.

"This has got to be a large carnivore."

"Maybe," Kehoe replied. "But no black bear around this time of year." He shrugged. "Maybe a mountain lion, but haven't seen one of those in years either, even a few miles out."

"Wolves?" Mitch asked.

"Nope, not anymore. We may get the occasional grey wandering in from Minnesota, Wisconsin, or Michigan. But they're too rare to be considered a threat." Kehoe pointed his chin at Hank. "And I'm damn sure this ain't a wolf kill anyway."

"Okay." Mitch looked around. "Where's the kid? Alfie?"

"Missing. But I found some bedding up here, plus some excrement. If I had to guess, I'd say the kid had been living up here."

"And he was just shitting on the floor." Melnick made a guttural sound of disgust in his throat.

Mitch continued to examine the body. There were scrapes on the bone consistent with teeth and claws, and at the lower end of the sternum something was embedded in the bone.

From his bag, he withdrew a pair of forceps and a small plastic jar and levered the shard free. He held it up.

Kehoe squinted. "Looks like a splinter."

Mitch continued to stare. *It did look like a splinter*, he thought. But it was shaped like a long talon, was dark brown, and had a grainy texture like wood rather than keratin that hair, nails, and claws were made of.

He dropped it into the jar, sealed it, but continued to stare at the thing. His mind leaped back to Ben Wainwright's notes and he was reminded of his descriptions of the kids, the wood-like growths covering them, plus their feral behavior.

"We need to find Alfie." He rose to his feet.

"Priority," Kehoe replied.

"You think the kid was carried off by whatever did this?" Melnick asked.

Mitch ignored the question. "And we also need to contact the CDC."

"What?" Melnick's mouth dropped open. "Why?"

"This reminds me of something Ben Wainright saw back in 1977—an infection from the mine. Gross deformities, abnormal aggressive behavior in children, and also several mutilations and deaths."

Melnick scoffed. "You got all that from a freaking splinter?" He frowned as he tilted his head. "Hey, wait a minute—you don't think the kid was carried off, do you?"

"That year, 1977…you're talking about Angel Syndrome,

right?" Kehoe asked.

Mitch nodded.

"Oh, for fucks sake. I wasn't mayor back then, but my predecessor gave me a rundown on notable events on his watch in the town and he talked about what happened back then in '77. The CDC came in, shut everything down, took a few people away for observation, and ruined the tourist trade for a decade." He shook his head. "So, excuse me if I don't break my neck to destroy Eldon's economy over a single wild animal death."

Mitch turned to Kehoe. "You said yourself it was unlikely to be a bear, wolf, or mountain lion."

Kehoe tilted his head. "I said it was unlikely, not impossible." He lifted his chin. "Doc, are you really saying a ten-year-old kid could do this? To his father?"

Mitch thought about it for a moment. "Yeah, I am."

"Bullshit," Melnick shot back. He turned to Kehoe. "I want answers, *real* answers supported by the evidence, and not conjecture based on some old notes from a guy that suffered from depression and was obviously suicidal."

Melnick turned and headed for the steps but paused at the top. "Sheriff, you run this, but keep it covert, because I do not want a panic. Understood?"

Kehoe nodded. "Of course, Mayor."

Melnick then faced Mitch. "Mitch, you assist."

Mitch sighed and watched the mayor disappear down the steps. He turned to Kehoe who just shrugged.

"What now?" Mitch asked.

"Analyse that fragment you found and let me know what you find." He swung his flashlight around one last time. "I'll get a team in here to investigate and put out a search on the kid."

The sheriff turned back and smiled crookedly. "But the mayor is right—we need to be sensible how we approach this. You start yelling *deformed kids, contamination,* or *mutilations*, and people get scared. Scared enough to panic and leave. No one wants to see cars packed up and people leaving town at the start of the tourist season. Sometimes they don't come back, and that's what kills small towns."

Mitch nodded. "Yeah, I hear you." He then pointed to the savaged body. "But a few more of these will kill it even quicker."

"Sure will, Doc. So, let's get to work." Kehoe nodded to the steps. "After you."

They went down the steps and just before Mitch headed to the front door, he held up a hand. "Wait a sec."

"What?" Kehoe called after him.

Mitch headed down the hall checking each room until he found the one he wanted—the washroom. In a glass on the basin were two toothbrushes, a large frayed one, and a smaller one with Iron Man on the handle. He grabbed both.

When he exited, he held them up to Kehoe. "DNA matching."

"Good thinking." The sheriff took one last look over his shoulder, pausing for a moment to let his eyes wander over the house's silent interior, and then shut the door.

CHAPTER 20

Mitch had sent the fragment he had pulled from Hank's chest off to a buddy in the military. Greg Samson did his training with Mitch, and like him had a medical background. He was in the Special Forces and he was one of the guys who had pulled what was left of him and his group from the battlefield in Syria. Afterward, Mitch left the service, but Greg went on to be retained in the biomedical section of the armed forces.

He joined a team in a hi-tech laboratory that was used to develop vaccines, antidotes, and prophylactics against a range of potential biological weapons their adversaries may or may not be developing.

If anyone could tell him what the hell he was dealing with, it was Greg Samson.

It was late, 9 pm, and Mitch was still in his office and hunched over his desk. In front of him were Wainright's files about the syndrome that affected Eldon back in the late seventies, and this time he pored over each page with a forensic intensity.

The contamination had come out of nowhere; one minute everything was normal and the next, the kids were getting sick.

He read more about the symptoms and became more and more convinced that the thing that had been hiding in Hank Ball's attic that attacked him and ate their cat was more than likely his ten-year-old son, Alfie.

He made summary notes as he read the documents, listing anything that he thought might be relevant or worth following up. When he finished, he sat back, used a hand to rake his hair back from his forehead, and read down his list of bullet points:
- Kids infected
- Angel Syndrome
- Symptoms—rash, hardening of epidermal skin layer, loss of appetite, psychotic behavior

- Johnson Nightbird

And finally:

- *Adotte Sakima*—the tree god

He sat staring at the old Native American's name and thought of the weird statue-like petrified structures in the museum that he had assisted in setting up. *Was there a connection?* he wondered.

"*Jesus!*" The phone suddenly ringing in the tomb-silent room made him jump inches from his seat. "Calm down, will you?" he ordered himself and grabbed up the phone.

"That you, Stitch?"

Mitch grinned from ear to ear upon hearing his friend's voice. *Stitch*—shortened from *Stitches*—was the nickname he was given when he was in the hospital and Greg had caught sight of him just after he regained consciousness—he was covered in bandages, tape, and more stitches than he could count, hence the name.

"Sure enough, Greg, good to hear from you, buddy." He sat back.

"Glad I caught you, what time is it there?" Greg asked.

Mitch checked his watch. "Now? Nine-thirty, not late."

"How's Eldon treating you? Is it as good as the town images I'm looking at on my screen right now?" Greg asked.

"It's better." Mitch then gave him a thumbnail overview of what the town was like, the people, and then what was going on. He finished with the retrieval of the claw, or tooth, or whatever it was, recovered from Hank Bell that he had sent him.

"Yeah, that's the weirdest damn thing ever," Greg replied.

"Was it human or animal?" Mitch asked.

Greg exhaled. "You know, Mitch, I'm not really sure. For a start, the sample you sent seemed to have all the hallmarks of very ancient, petrified wood, and therefore should have been devoid of DNA. But it wasn't. When I extracted out the DNA fragments, I found that it was like a mish-mash of different kinds of things—a chimera."

"*Chimera,*" Mitch repeated the word. He knew the term; in Greek mythology, a chimera was a monstrous, fire-breathing hybrid creature with the parts of more than one animal, such as lion, goat, and snake. But in modern medical terms, a chimera was a single organism made up of cells from two or more individuals. That meant it contained two sets of DNA with the entire code to make two separate organisms.

"You mean it was a mix of two people's DNA, like a father and son, right?" Mitch asked.

"No, and normally about this time I'd be checking to make sure this wasn't an elaborate prank, but now I don't think the sample you gave me could be faked. The thing about DNA is it's the building blocks for everything organic and every cell contains the good old familiar double helix twisted ladder. Both animal DNA and plant DNA molecules are made from the same four chemical building blocks called nucleotides."

"Yeah, got that." Mitch sat forward and meshed his fingers.

Greg went on. "But, the difference between mammalian or any animal DNA and plant DNA is how the four nucleotides in the DNA are arranged. It's their sequence that determines which proteins will be made. The way the nucleotides are arranged, and the information they encode, decides whether the organism will produce scales or leaves, legs or stalk, skin or bark."

"Oka-*aaay*." Mitch waited.

"Mitch, this damn thing is a chimera of totally separate species' DNA. It has in its scrambled code elements in the helix that are nucleotide signatures for both mammalian and plant DNA." He scoffed. "I'm looking right at it, and I still don't believe what I'm seeing."

Greg sounded like he sat forward. "Listen, Mitch, don't quote me on this, but it looks like it's halfway on a transition. One seems to be turning into the other—plant to animal, or animal to plant. I can't tell which."

Mitch felt his stomach flip when he remembered Wainright's notes about the Billy Allison kid he described and his metamorphosis.

He gripped the phone harder. "Greg, this is important—the mammalian DNA, *was it once human?*"

The military scientist paused for a moment. "It might have been, yeah, once."

Mitch sat back and shut his eyes. He bet his last dollar that thing came from the kid, Alfie. That somehow, he had been transformed or was transforming…into something else. But into what?

Mitch felt like his brain was fried and couldn't think

straight. "Thanks, Greg, I gotta go. But as always, you're a big help to me."

"Hey, wait a minute," Greg shot back. "Where did it come from? This thing is a medical anomaly of outstanding importance. I need to know more."

Mitch nodded. "I know, I know. But not right now. I've got to sort this out in my head first." He took a deep breath. "One more thing—please keep this to yourself for now, okay?"

"Yeah, sure, okay. Just let me know if you need anything else. I'm always here for you, bud," Greg said. "Just don't forget us here in Nebraska. Got a cold beer waiting with your name on it."

"Okay, and thanks, Greg…" A sudden thought came to him. "…Wait, there is something that might fill in some of the missing pieces to this puzzle. Do you still have your contacts at the CDC?"

"Yeah, sure, a couple of good people I know very well. They're still in there. What is it?" Greg asked.

"That's great. Look, I need you to find out something for me. Back in 1977, the previous doctor here reported an outbreak of something here in Eldon, and the CDC came and transferred all of the infected people to some medical facility. I can't find any record of them ever returning. Or where they ever ended up."

"That's really weird," Greg replied. "You want me to see if I can find them?"

"Yeah, find them, and find out what happened to them." Mitch suddenly felt he had some forward motion. "It might help me understand what I'm dealing with now."

"I'm on it, buddy, leave it with me," Greg replied.

Mitch hung up and rubbed his eyes with the heels of his hands. He blinked a moment and then his eyes slid to the notes he had written. Wainright had hypothesized that the source of the contamination was the mine. He'd check that out with the sheriff first thing tomorrow.

He then picked up the list he had written and saw the Native American's name again: *Johnson Nightbird.*

He remembered what Greg had told him, that it looked like the mammalian DNA, Alfie's, was transitioning into something else, something that was part plant and part human. And it looked like petrified wood.

The last line he had on his list was an ancient word: *Adotte Sakima.*

"The tree god," he whispered.

CHAPTER 21

"What is it, Mitch?" Sheriff Kehoe's voice was strained with exasperation.

Mitch drove with one hand and held the phone to his ear. He always planned to get a hands-free answering in the car but, well, it'll never happen. "Hi, Dan, we need to check something out, right now."

Kehoe sighed. "Little snowed under here, Doc, is it…?"

"Yeah, it is important," Mitch cut in. "Ben Wainright said he believed a lot of the problems they had back in 1977 came from the mine. We need to check it out."

Kehoe sighed. "Now?"

"Yes please. This could be important in understanding what happened to Hank. And Alfie." Mitch waited. And waited.

And then.

"Okay, I'm not far from you. But do *not* go into that mine until I get there. You got that, Doc?" Kehoe warned.

"Sure, sure," Mitch said distractedly.

Mitch arrived at the mine turnoff and powered up the rutted track until he got to the fencing and pulled over. He sat in the car for several minutes, and then decided to take a quick look. After all, he promised not to go *into* the mine, but not to just stand outside and check things out.

He retraced his steps to get to the main shaft area and as he breached the hilltop was stopped in his tracks.

"Holy crap." He scoffed. "Oasis is right."

"*Hey*."

Mitch cringed at the stern voice. He turned slowly to see the sheriff striding up the track.

"You don't take advice easily, do you, Doc?" Kehoe shook his head. "Remember what killed the cat."

"Furballs?" Mitch grinned. "You said do not go *into* the mine, right?" He turned back to the mine and pointed as he walked slowly up to the large, green-tinged pond. "Look at this.

This wasn't here when I checked it out only a few weeks back. And there's even more trees."

"Don't get too close," Kehoe said. He sniffed. "Smells like the ocean at low tide."

Mitch agreed. "Could be some methane residue that was in with the limestone, I guess. Looks fairly clear though. But that's exactly what Ben…" He stopped, remembering what else Wainright had included in his notes. "Let's take a look."

He walked closer to the pond edge and fished in his pocket for the small plastic sample jar he had brought with him. He crouched, unscrewed the lid and dipped it in, half filling it.

Mitch held it up toward the sun and then shook it. "No obvious particular matter, except for a slight green color. But could be chemical residue, plant staining, maybe even bacterial, fungal, or even viral." He sniffed it. "Yep, something a little unpleasant in there." He screwed the cap on.

Kehoe looked around. "Amazing what a little water will do. Last I saw this place a few years back, it was just a dusty, dry nothing. Now it looks like somewhere I'd like to bring the family on a picnic."

"Yeah, well, I wouldn't do that right now." Mitch stood. "I'm going to look at this under a microscope. See if there's anything toxic hiding in it."

Kehoe's radio squawked.

"Sheriff?"

He lifted the handset. "What is it, Anderson?"

"Sheriff, I'm down at Harlen Bimford's shop. Something you might want to see," Deputy Pete Anderson replied.

"Pete, I'm kinda busy right now. What is it?" Kehoe turned away.

"Best if you come take a look. It's not good," Anderson replied.

Kehoe sighed. "Okay, Pete, on my way." He turned. "We done here, Doc?"

"Yeah." Mitch turned about. "Just might be best to get some new signs made up to keep people out of the water."

"Good idea, you do it. Public health order. And send the bill to the council." Kehoe turned back to the track and headed down. He spoke over his shoulder. "And let me know if you find anything interesting in the water."

Mitch watched him go for a moment until he disappeared behind some of the trees further down. He turned back to the mine mouth. The sun beat down on the shimmering, cool water, and he knew it would have been irresistible to him if he was a kid. Heck, as an adult, he felt like diving in right now.

He lifted his gaze from the water. Beyond the pond, the mine mouth where the water had obviously welled up from was as dark and ominous as ever. He stared into its mysterious blackness, and after a moment, his eyes started to play tricks and see movement and the twin dot glow of nocturnal eyes staring back at him. The hair rose on the back of his neck.

"And that's it for me."

Mitch headed back to his car.

*****

Kehoe pulled up out front of Bimford's soda and drug store to see his deputy, Pete Anderson, waiting out front. The young man waved and briefly looked back over his shoulder in through the glass window before heading toward the cruiser.

Kehoe nodded. "What is it, Pete?"

"Wish I could describe it. But I thought best if you see yourself." He turned and put a hand on the door.

Kehoe followed him. "Is Harlen okay?"

"Yeah, he's fine, just a little shook up." Anderson pushed open the shop door, making a small bell tinkle. "Harlen, it's me again, Deputy Pete. I've got the sheriff here."

"Dan, is that you?"

Kehoe followed the voice. "I'm here, Harlen, how you doin'?"

"I'm okay, I guess."

Kehoe found the man sitting in a chair. Across his knees was a cracked shotgun, and the man's shirt was all torn up.

Kehoe's brows knitted as he looked the old man over and slowly reached out a hand. "Take that for you, Harlen?"

Bimford handed over the shotgun.

"What happened?" Kehoe asked.

"Aw, goddamn Buford attacked me." He stared straight ahead. "Least I think it was him." He looked up at the sheriff, his eyes glassy. "Had that dog eight years. He loved me. And I loved him." His eyes welled up. "I shot him. Had to."

"Where is he?" Kehoe knew the man's dog, Buford. He was one of the not very bright hounds that just wanted to bark at squirrels, lay by a fire, and beg for food. And Harlen was right, it adored him and would never have attacked him.

"This here is what he shot." Deputy Anderson went to a tarpaulin spread over a lump half hidden by some of the racks and drew it back.

Kehoe stood and stared for ten seconds as he tried to make sense of the thing. The creature was basically dog-shaped, but instead of fur it looked to be covered in splinters.

Where the head should have been was just a chunk of something that was ragged and open like a split log, and spiked teeth went from the tip all the way down the gullet that extended even down into the muscular neck.

Around the outside of the neck and embedded into it was a dog collar just showing.

Kehoe looked along the animal's body—there was a fist-sized hole in the shoulder, and inside the torso he could see even the muscles and internal organs had the same fibrous, woody texture.

He looked up. "What the hell happened to him, Harlen? How'd he get like this?"

"I don't know, Sheriff. He looked kinda strange last night before bed, but he slept all through. When I woke up, I couldn't find him. Then this thing jumped out and attacked me." Harlen suddenly looked hopeful. "Hey, maybe it ain't him."

Kehoe carefully touched one of the sharp teeth that looked more like a long rose thorn. He remembered the attack on Hank and the shard they found stuck in the body—*could this thing have done it?* he wondered.

"You say Buford was okay last night?" he asked.

"Seemed a bit tired but he looked fine," Harlen replied wearily.

Kehoe nodded. The timeline didn't match up. He got to his feet and kicked the dog's body with the toe of his boot. It was hard, solid, and definitely dead.

Harlen sniffed wetly. "Maybe that thing attacked Buford. And ate him."

Kehoe nodded but glanced back at the familiar collar. "We'll take care of it." He patted the man's shoulder and thought he felt a sport of hardness under his shirt. He gently took hold of the man's collar and carefully peeled it back. He saw Harlen had some sort of pebbly rash there.

"You feelin' okay, Harlen?" He let the collar go and wiped his hand on his pants.

Harlen looked up. "I probably just shot my best dog so not really, Sheriff."

Kehoe nodded. "Okay, we'll take care of this. But I want you to do something for me. I want you to go and see the new doctor in town, and today, okay?"

The old man nodded distractedly.

"Good man." Kehoe turned to his deputy. "Pete, let's get this out of here. It goes in your trunk."

CHAPTER 22

Mitch sat at his desk with a strong light bent over a muscle-strainingly thick encyclopedia of North American plant pollens, spores, and seeds. He had used the high-resolution microscope camera to take images of some of the flora and fauna he found in the water sample, and there were several of them giving him trouble tracking down their description in the book.

Unfortunately, they seemed to be the ones that might be giving the water its odd, deep green hue.

"Could that be a seed?" he asked the quiet room as he spotted something else interesting. But it seemed far too small, and even with his top magnification, it stayed only dust-speck sized.

He did remember from Cindy's gardening days that some varieties of epiphytic orchids created seeds that were only 1/300th of an inch or just 85 micrometers. Microscopic when you consider that a typical grain of salt is nearly four times bigger at around 300 micrometers.

But this seed was even smaller than that. Mitch sighed, rubbed his eyes, and sat back. This seed, along with the spores, was beyond his encyclopedia's capabilities. There were several good botanical universities he could send the samples off to get a definitive answer. But there was also the next best, and far faster option—ask Doctor Google.

He uploaded the image of the spore and seed and ran a search on them. After a few seconds, it found a near-perfect match, for the spore at least. As Mitch read, his brows came together.

"You gotta be shitting me."

There was an article published in the *Frontiers in Plant Science* where a team of scientists from the Paleontological Institute and Museum at the University of Zürich had found plant spores that pushed back everything we know about the evolution of plants.

They had found angiosperm-like pollen fragments that dated back to the Middle Triassic, approximately 240 million years ago, that suggested flowering plants may have evolved much earlier than originally believed.

Mitch looked from the images the scientific team had captured and back to his—the shape and structures were the same, and the only real differences were that their pollen spore was a desiccated fossil, and his was hydrated, colorful, and alive.

He then focused on the microscopic seed—this remained a mystery. However, there was one suggestion, and the only clue was from an impression in some Devonian period slate for something similar. And that was from around 400 million years ago and came from the very first seed-bearing plants.

"The seed of the first tree," he whispered.

"Doctor Taylor, *Mitch…*"

Shelly's voice from the reception area rose in pitch and Mitch emerged from his practice rooms.

"What is it, Shell…?" Mitch frowned as Sheriff Kehoe and his deputy held a tarpaulin sheet between them with something heavy in it. "What the hell is this?"

"Like your opinion on something, Doc." Kehoe paused. "Where to?"

"Where? *Ah…*" Mitch might have made them take it back outside but he could see the worry on the sheriff's face. He looked around. "In the surgery room." He went and pushed another door open, which had a steel bench inside and was a pristine white.

Kehoe and Deputy Anderson carried the thing in and hefted it up onto the bench. Kehoe then flipped the cover back. He didn't say a word, just looked from the thing to Mitch with his arms folded.

"Holy shit." Mitch lifted a hand to it, then stopped. He moved to a shelf and grabbed some disposable gloves, then tossed the box to Kehoe. He pulled them on and approached the thing.

"What is it?" he asked.

Kehoe snapped on the gloves and went to the other end of the creature. He carefully reached along the spiked and splintery-looking neck and lifted something. Mitch craned forward and saw it was a dog collar.

"I believe this is, was, Buford, Harlen Bimford's faithful old hound." Kehoe looked up. "It attacked him."

Mitch peered inside the shotgun wound in its side. He snorted softly. "Even the organs look petrified." He looked up. "You said this thing was alive?"

Kehoe nodded. "According to Harlen. It attacked him and he had to shoot it."

The sheriff peeled off his gloves. "Over to you, Doc." He nodded to his deputy and they headed for the door.

"Hey, wait a minute. You can't drop this on me and then just back out." Mitch began to follow them.

Kehoe turned at the door. "You're the coroner as well, Mitch. Plus, the closest thing we've got to an onsite forensic pathologist. It's got to be you." He went out. "Let me know what you find."

The door closed behind them and Shelly came in, watching them go for a moment. She turned. "I used to date Pete Anderson." She dragged her eyes away from the young man to alight on the deformed dog. "What's that?"

Mitch's sigh turned into a groan. "Right now? Just more work."

*****

Mitch washed his hands, dried them on a towel, and turned back to old Buford's body. He had needed to use an electric bone saw during the autopsy, and on completion still had no idea how a biological entity could reorganize itself so completely.

Mitch suddenly had a hunch, grabbed the saw, severed the stomach and intestines, and set to opening the now leathery bag of a gut. He laid them open and sorted through their contents.

"*Phew*." He grimaced and held his breath as the gases rose from the pile—in amongst the mush was dog food, some of Harlen Bimford's shirt, and also plenty of liquid. But there was no flesh in the stomach or the intestines that might have belonged to Hank Bell.

He sighed. "So, I can rule you out as a suspect."

Mitch used a large syringe to take a sample of the liquid and placed it under his microscope.

"Hmm." He enlarged the view and adjusted the overhead light—sure enough, there were the tiny flecks of the flora he had seen in the water sample from the mine pool.

"Well, well, well."

He looked back over his shoulder at the hound's deformed body and remembered what his friend, Greg, had told him—that the people seemed to be undergoing some sort of transitional process. He continued to stare at Buford—was this the end stage? Or were there more changes yet to occur?

Scientific curiosity gnawed at him. He wondered whether the animal had been up to the mine and had swum in or drunk the water. Or had he ingested the water flora somehow, somewhere else. *Harlen might know*, he guessed. *Or he might not.*

A rustling from behind made him turn to see Willard the greasy black rat chewing on the edge of his newspaper. Willard stopped and stared back at him through the bars of his cage with tiny red eyes like polished glass.

"Wasn't my idea, buddy."

Mitch had come back into his office a few days back to Shelly announcing the rat had been caught. Thinking back now, he couldn't remember whether he said he wanted him *caught* or *caught and taken away*. So the rat, Willard, had taken up residence. For now.

Mitch continued to watch the little animal for a moment before he slowly turned to where he had set up his testing station and racks of test tubes. One of them still contained the greenish water he had collected from the mine pond.

He turned back to the rat. "Hey, Willard, want to finally be useful and help me with a little experiment?"

The rat stared back, its nose twitching.

"I'll take that as a yes." He crossed to the test tube rack and also grabbed up a small stopper. Crossing back to the rat's cage, he used the stopper to draw up some of the greenish fluid and then squirted it into Willard's drinking water.

After a moment, the entire mixture was green, and the rat's nose twitched as if it had a life of its own and soon pointed toward the water. Willard went and immediately drank some of the fluid.

"Good boy." Mitch smiled then quickly went to a notebook and jotted down some observations and the time. He turned, pulled out his phone, and took several pictures of the small animal.

He pointed with his pen. "Okay, Master Splinter, let me know if there are any changes, okay?"

The phone rang, and Mitch lifted it while keeping his eyes on the rat. "Mitch Taylor."

"Mitch, Greg." Greg Samson didn't sound his usual cheery self.

"Hi, Greg, everything okay?" Mitch asked.

"Hey, thanks for throwing me down the rabbit hole. By the way, I don't care what you say, I'm coming to Eldon," he replied.

"What, why, what happened?" Mitch asked.

"I did as you asked and made some gentle little requests into the CDC to some of my old buddies. I got a few documents, but for the most part everything is classified and well above my, or my contacts', paygrade. But we did get some hits." He scoffed softly. "You ready for this?'

"Yes and no," Mitch replied. "You're scaring me but go on."

Mitch heard what sounded like pages being folded or turned. Then Greg exhaled.

"Okay, they managed to obtain some research notes and photographs from the afflicted group that was brought in from Eldon, Oakland Count, Missouri, in August 1977…"

"Wait, that's what they called them? *Afflicted*?" Mitch asked.

"Yep, it's in their notes." He went on. "There were eight families and several individual children whose parents had vanished. Plus, some adults with children missing and unaccounted for."

"Where are they now? Still there?" Mitch asked, intrigued.

"Maybe they are, but there's no record of where they were taken in any of the documents I was given. My contacts will do some more digging, but don't hold your breath," he replied. "Mitch, you remember when I said that the DNA samples you gave me exhibited something that might or might not have been transitioning from plant to animal or vice versa?"

Mitch gripped the handset, hard. "Yes, of course. How could I forget?"

"Well, that transitioning moved on considerably in these afflicted people. It was some sort of contagion that seemed to work on both the cellular and genetic level, altering the DNA structure completely. And Mitch, it does it at an unprecedented and escalating pace."

"What is it? Describe what you're looking at." Mitch felt his heart racing in his chest.

"I've got photographs. Not great resolution given they were taken in the seventies, but at least they're in color." He sighed. "Jesus, Mitch, these poor souls, they aren't even human anymore."

"I don't… I don't understand what that means." Mitch felt a throbbing headache coming on.

"There's pictures of some of the kids here with things growing out of their backs that look like coral. Some look like small creatures covered in splinters, and others are just covered over in what looks like shell carapace," Greg replied.

"A nightmare." Mitch straightened. "Exactly like Buford."

"Who?" Greg asked.

"A dog in town. It attacked its owner, and it had changed. It was deformed by all these extraneous growths, internally and externally." Mitch tried to get his head around *that* alteration happening to a human. "Horrifying."

"Yeah, it is, but that's not the worst of it," Greg replied. "This is gonna sound crazy, but it looked like some of the adults were transitioning into, and I'll read what they've written here: *arboreal entities*."

"*Arboreal entities…*" Mitch laughed but with little humor. "*Trees*."

"Mitch, I'm looking at the transitional pictures of humans that are turning to wood. And the last few pictures have notes attached that say the subjects were still alive. And the worst thing was they were carnivorous—apparently, they needed the nutrients from flesh and blood to survive. That's your damn nightmare right there."

"Holy shit." Mitch couldn't get his head around it.

"Hold a minute." Greg sounded like he leaned away, then came back. "I've taken a picture of this last photograph and am sending it to your phone, right, *now*."

Mitch reached for his phone and in just another second it pinged with a message from Greg. He opened it, and before him was a picture of several people huddled together holding onto each other and between them fibrous-looking roots intertwining their group.

On the face of the person closest, he could just make out the expression of agony or torment. It was as if they were all being trapped within this petrifying form for eternity, and they knew it.

"I've seen this before," Mitch breathed out.

"Where?" Greg asked quickly.

"The museum here in town," Mitch replied. "Apparently, a group of these petrified statues were dug out of the mine or a tunnel offshoot, over 100 years ago. You know what? When I first saw them, I knew the details were too perfect."

"I want to see them," Greg whispered.

Mitch cast his mind back. "The museum curator thought that they were statues carved from some sort of unidentifiable petrified wood. And that someone had taken them into the mine or the caves there, long, long ago. But what if they weren't statues at all? What if they were infected people who walked in there and spent the last days of their lives turning into these things down in the darkness?"

"Mitch, that's it, I'm dropping everything and coming over. This is the most confounding thing I have ever heard of." Greg's voice sped up. "We should also inform the CDC, and not just my buddies but the formal channels. Let them—"

"No, we can't." Mitch sighed. "No CDC, not yet anyway. The mayor here is adamant we do not involve the authorities until we know more. He told me last time, in '77, it nearly devastated the town. Besides, there's only been a few outbreaks, and we think we have it under control."

"Bullshit, we bring them in," Greg urged. "They have far better resources than we do."

"They do, but we don't call them in yet." Mitch rubbed his eyes with his thumb and forefinger. "Just remember, this is my home now, and I've got to work with these people."

"Fine, I get it, you don't want to lose your job. But I'm still coming over," Greg replied. "The address you gave me for the medical practice you're working at is all I've got. So, I come there first?"

"I won't be here," Mitch said.

"Okay, so, where will I meet you?" Greg sounded confused. "Don't freeze me out of this, Mitch."

"No, I need your help. But we keep everything low key from now on." He turned away from the desk. "I need to see an expert, and someone who seemed to have a lot of knowledge about these events."

"Who, where?" Greg asked.

"Red Rock, Oklahoma. I'm going to try and track down a Nightbird. You can meet me there," Mitch replied.

"Sounds intriguing. Tomorrow afternoon?" he asked.

"Yep, call me when you get in," Mitch replied.

The pair exchanged a few more details, and then Mitch hung up. He was glad Greg would be joining him. The guy was a rock, a clear-headed thinker, and would also be damn good company. And right now, he felt he needed the support.

He stood thinking for a moment more before a rustling from the cage on the shelf behind him drew his attention.

Mitch walked slowly toward the cage and stared in at the small animal—the once greasy-looking fur of the dark rat was now spiky-looking toward its rear and the head was partially obscured by a lumpy protrusion over the brow.

From its back, things like branches of coral extended, and on seeing Mitch so close it leaped at the bars of the cage, making the entire enclosure rattle.

"Whoa there, little guy." Mitch took a step back.

The rat had stopped its inquisitive sniffing and the ever-twitching nose had also stopped moving. It simply sat glaring at Mitch, its body pulsing in and out with fast breaths.

"Transitional," he said, repeating Greg's analysis. "And what will you transition to, Willard?" he asked and leaned forward.

The rat's response was to leap at the cage bars again. Mitch could see that the cereal grains he had given it were now largely untouched so he went to his office icebox, took out his ham sandwich, and pulled free a slice of the meat. He went back to the cage and dropped it between the bars.

The rat set upon it instantly. Mitch lowered himself down

and watched Willard devour the meat. It held it in its tiny hands and he saw that the mouth that had once had normally ratty chisel-shaped incisors at the front now looked like it belonged to some sort of viper.

After another moment, the entire piece was gone.

A chaotic metabolism in flux needs fuel, Mitch observed.

In response to that food, the rat's body seemed to balloon, and the coral branching from its back grew another inch into wing-shaped structures. He observed them filling with blood.

"What are they for, little guy?"

Mitch turned away to gather up a few things for his trip. He quickly did an Internet scan of Red Rock and of some local hotels he could potentially stay at, and then stood thinking about what else he would need or should do.

"Oh." He let his bag and folders slide back onto the desktop and snatched up the phone.

"Hi, Karen." He wanted to sound calm and upbeat even though he felt a pall of doom being pulled across them. But just hearing her voice made him feel…good.

"Hi back," she said. "Watcha doin'?"

He smiled. "Just heading out of town for a few days, medical conference."

"Sounds boring, where is it?" she asked.

"Probably will be." He smiled brokenly. "It's in Red Rock."

She chuckled. "Really? Red Rock? Have you been there before?"

"No, have you?" he asked, now wondering whether he should have told her somewhere else, more medical conferency sounding.

"Well, great sunsets, good hiking, and the best food in the state at the Red Rock Canyon Café. But it has a population of only around 290 people, so it's very quiet."

"Quiet is good; it is a work thing, you know." He checked his watch. "Wish you were coming. That'd make it less boring," he said and felt his face redden at the forwardness of the suggestion.

She didn't reply and he immediately regretted saying it. "Sorry," he added.

"Don't be," she said softly. "I like you, Mitch, but let's just take it slow, okay?"

"Yeah, yeah. Can I see you when I get back?" He held his breath.

"Okay. And one more thing." She sounded like she smiled. "Wish I was coming too." She rang off.

Mitch looked skyward. "Thank you." He gathered up his gear again.

On his way to the door, he cast a glance at the rat and paused. "What am I supposed to do with you? I can't exactly let you loose, can I?"

Mitch quickly went to the icebox, grabbed the rest of his sandwich, and then dumped the entire thing in through the top of the cage.

"That'll keep you going until I get back. And when I do, I'm gonna make you a star."

He then threw a fire blanket over the cage, hopefully damping down the smell and sound in the event Shelly poked her head in. He peeked in again and saw that the rat was glaring back at him, but this time its once beady, red eyes now glowed yellow.

"*Yeesh.*" He dropped the blanket back down.

Mitch Taylor took one last look around and then went out the door fast.

*****

The silence of Mitch's office was soon broken by the sound of scrabbling, and then a grinding, followed by a metallic *plink*. After another few moments, there came another, and then another.

One by one, the bars of the cage were being broken off or bent away. And then the fire blanket was moved aside.

CHAPTER 23

The taxi turned off Fir Street at the huge luminous green sign that glowed even in the sunshine and announced they'd arrived at the Perry Holiday Inn.

Perry was the closest town Mitch could get to Red Rock, and given they were only a few miles from the town center, it'd do just fine. Mitch thanked the driver, tipped him, and then stepped out into blistering sunshine.

"Ouch." He flipped his collar up from the burn. He squinted and turned slowly. Across the road was an Exxon gas station and then beyond that, miles and miles of flat, dry, and scrubby land.

He knew he was taking a gamble as he had no way to locate the ancient Native American, or even find out if he was still alive. But he knew being here in the place that was the reservation of the Missouria Otoe Native Americans, and the last place he had be known to inhabit, then if he wasn't here, he probably wouldn't find him anywhere.

Mitch hefted his single bag onto his shoulder and headed into the inn's gleaming marble and glass reservation area.

The man's grin behind the counter was a mile wide and he was greeted like an old friend, and immediately given a room upgrade when he identified himself as a doctor.

As he waited for his room key, his phone buzzed, and he grinned when he saw the name.

"Hi, Greg, you got here okay? I'm at the Holiday Inn, where are you at?" Mitch was handed his room key, nodded his thanks, and turned to look out through the glass doors.

"Hey, Stitch, I'm at the Wyndam Perry, about half a mile down the road from you," Greg replied. "What's the plan?"

"I'm just checking in, then I'll grab a quick shower and we should meet up. What's your bar look like?" Mitch looked along the corridor to the small open area of the Holiday Inn bar. He swore he saw tumbleweeds blowing through it.

"Not bad, plus I think I see free bar snacks." Greg chuckled. "Also…"

"Stop there, you had me at *free bar snacks*." Mitch checked his watch. "Be there in under an hour." He started up the steps to his room but paused. He jogged back to the desk.

The cheery-faced check-in clerk raised his eyebrows and continued to smile. "Can I help you?"

"Yeah, maybe. Do you know a Native American man by the name of Johnson Nightbird?"

His smile widened. "What's he done now?"

"I'll take that as a yes, and also that he's still alive." Mitch felt relieved. "I'm a doctor from Eldon and just wanted to ask him some questions about some consulting work he did for our museum a while back. Might need his services again."

The clerk pulled out a notepad. "I'm Otoe too. Old 'J.N.' is a legend around these parts. Knows everything about everything." He leaned forward. "He's a shaman, you know."

"A wizard?" Mitch asked.

"More like a spirit talker and wise man. But he's a powerful one." He began to write on the notepad but paused to look up. "You've got a car, right?"

Mitch nodded.

"Good, then you turn right on the 64, then left onto the 77 and stay on that for about 12 miles until you get to the 15." He drew a detailed diagram as he spoke. "Then you head along that toward the settlement of Red Rock itself. But, most importantly, just before you get there, turn left onto the 160."

Mitch traced the route with his finger and nodded, following it easily. The clerk went on.

"About half a mile along the 160, you'll come to a small turn-off with a mailbox that has a carved eagle on top. Take it and follow that all the way to Johnson Nightbird's place. It's right on the edge of Red Rock Canyon Creek."

The clerk straightened, smiling. "He doesn't have a phone and is a little short-tempered these days. So, if you don't get shot in the first few seconds, remember to say hello to him from Jimmy at the Inn."

Mitch chuckled. "You're joking, right?"

Jimmy continued to smile.

*****

"Cheers. To good days." Greg clinked his beer glass up against Mitch's.

"And even better ones to come," Mitch replied, and then they both sipped.

"So how are you these days, Mitch? I mean, really?" Greg watched him.

Mitch knew what he was getting at. After Syria, he had carried around a lot of guilt, blaming himself for walking his team into an ambush and also for the loss of the Kurdish woman.

Then Cindy lifted him out of his dark days only to die of cancer. His depression came down on him like a ton of bricks, and he began to believe he had poison touch syndrome, where anyone he loved would die.

"I'm good. In fact, *real* good these days. Eldon has, *ah*, exceeded my expectations." He lifted his glass in a toast.

Greg grinned. "Oh, that good, *huh*? Who is she then?"

"No one really. Just the vice mayor, is all." He chuckled. "We're just friends, but, who knows, she's pretty cool."

"Pretty cool or pretty hot?" Greg pressed.

Mitch nodded. "Both."

"I look forward to meeting her." He put his glass down. "Now tell me why you raced out of Eldon like your hair was on fire. What's the rush, and what the hell is with those people back in the seventies that suffered some weird, never heard of before, disfiguring infection?"

"That's just it—I think it *has* been heard of before. Maybe many times. We just didn't recognise it, or the time span was too great," Mitch replied. He sat forward, talking softer. "And in fact, I think whatever this infection is, it has happened many times in our history."

"And what does that have to do with Red Rock?" Greg asked.

"There's someone here who knows more about it than we do." Mitch pulled out his phone with the picture of the people becoming petrified and turned it around. "This is Angel Syndrome, which as far as I know hasn't affected anyone here just yet. Or at least none that I know of. But it did back in the seventies. And I believe it also happened long ago."

"The museum artifacts?" Greg's brows went up.

"Yeah, these guys." Mitch changed the picture to the petrified people in the museum. "This image of a family group was found in the depths of some caves below the town." Mitch handed Greg the phone.

Greg frowned as he swiped between the ancient statues and the people in the CDC images.

"Almost identical." He looked up. "When?"

"They were found at the turn of the century. But the real kicker is they've been dated to around 12,000 years ago." Mitch scoffed softly. "Whatever is going on, has been going on for thousands of years."

"Could be something in the indigenous animal population that surfaces seasonally, but on a long cycle. Did you know that armadillos were found to spread Hanson's disease, leprosy? In the Gulf states, some mating seasons the little bastards would wander closer to human populations, and bingo, people were catching the disease. Was a mystery how every second year, or decade, there'd be outbreaks, and it was only when they tested the local animals that they found their biological reservoir."

"Interesting. Never thought about that," Mitch mused.

Greg shrugged. "Well, thank God you don't have any outbreaks now."

"Maybe we don't have any obvious outbreaks, *yet*. That is, unless we head them off somehow." Mitch shrugged. "The sheriff is barricading off the mine, so hopefully we can keep people out and away from the water. But there's an old Native American called Johnson Nightbird who described the infection to the museum. He was in Eldon back in the seventies. He also said that the people had become *servants of Adotte Sakima*—the tree god."

Greg sat back slowly. "I don't understand."

Mitch shrugged. "That makes two of us. It's somehow all connected but I don't know how. And that's why we need to talk to him."

"And I'm guessing why we're here." Greg drained his beer and put the bottle down. "So, what do you hope to find out from this Nightbird?"

Mitch shook his head as he stared into his beer. "I don't

know yet. But I do know that the Otoe-Missouria tribe has been in this area for thousands of years and are one of the oldest in the country. Maybe entwined in one of their legends is an answer, or a clue, or something that can give us an idea of what it is we're dealing with."

"Well, sooner or later, you're going to have to bring in the CDC. My contacts in there were a little suspicious about why I wanted to dig those old cases up." He stood with his empty bottle. "Another?"

"Sure." Mitch drained his own drink. "Just remember, the mayor wants it handled locally for now. I'll play by his rules for a little longer."

"Okay, you've got to do that. But keep in mind, the CDC has national and international expertise. Plus, they *must* know something about this Angel Syndrome as they've dealt with it before."

Mitch looked up and shook his head. "No, they dealt with it by simply locking it away." He scoffed. "And what happened to all the children? Did they die or become petrified like their parents? Or are they still alive somewhere?"

"Mitch, we've both worked for the military and know what a tripwire is for. They asked me a hellova lot of questions about my basic searches. I kinda got the feeling if I asked any more, I'd set off some alarms and then someone is going to show up and start asking me, *us*, a lot more questions. Are you ready for that?"

Mitch shook his head. "No, not yet. I still don't understand what it is I've found or even what I'm looking for." He smiled. "And that's why I want to speak to this old Otoe elder."

"Did you make an appointment?" Greg asked.

"Nope. And only just found out where he lives an hour ago," Mitch replied.

"Hope he speaks to us. You better take him something… I dunno, like a house-warming present." Greg grinned.

"Good idea." Mitch went to the bar and bought a carton of cigarettes. He settled on Marlboro. He slid them on the table and Greg picked them up, cocking an eyebrow.

"Marlboro? Seriously? Is that a good idea? Don't cowboys smoke those?" He chuckled.

"*Pfft*, how old are you, 80? They retired the Marlboro Man

decades ago." Mitch shrugged. "If he doesn't smoke, he can give them away." Mitch finished his second drink and stood. "Just don't tell anyone a doctor is handing out cigarettes."

"I'm sure he'd prefer a bag of kale and a scented candle," Greg laughed.

"Even I'd shoot me for that sort of gift. Let's head out early tomorrow, 6:30 am, I'll pick you up. Should only take us an hour to get there, and hopefully track the old guy down."

Greg toasted his friend. "May you live in interesting times."

Mitch grinned. "Isn't that an old curse?"

*****

Mitch slowed as he spotted Greg standing out front of his hotel. The military medical man jumped into the rental.

"Let's go find ourselves a nightbird," he said as he buckled up.

Mitch followed the instructions given to him by his desk clerk and headed firstly out across flat highway for several miles toward a line of ragged, low-lying hills.

As they left the main highway that held a lot of the gas stations, hotels, and malls, they saw nature reclaim the landscape, where concrete turned to trees, waving grasses, and exposed pink stone.

It also meant that the roads became less smooth, and in no time, they were traveling along tracks with deep potholes that tested their suspension and jarred them to their back teeth.

"There." Mitch pointed through the windscreen.

It was a mailbox with an American bald eagle carving on top. There was no name or number on it, and Mitch guessed you just had to know whose it was. And you would if you lived out here.

Mitch turned slowly onto the path and headed on up.

"Should be only a few hundred yards now. Keep a lookout for a house. Or an old guy with a shotgun." Mitch chuckled as he drove about ten miles per hour as both men scanned the forest for a sign of Johnson Nightbird's dwelling place.

Then they passed through a large stand of trees and saw just up ahead nestled in among some huge trunks there was a cabin. Smoke curled from a stone chimney and the yard was strewn with automobiles, some were the color of earth as all their paint had rusted away, and another looking like someone was attempting to either take it apart or put it back together.

"This must be the place," Greg said.

Beside the house was a pile of chopped firewood six feet high.

"This guy is supposed to be in his late 70s and chopped all that wood himself?" Mitch observed. "Impressive."

"They must make 'em tough out here," Greg replied.

They pushed open their doors and stood in the pleasant, dappled sunshine.

Mitch drew in a deep breath of clean air until the rifle shot made both of the ex-military men crouch and reach for sidearms they didn't carry anymore.

"*Hold your fire*," Mitch yelled.

The pair moved forward with their hands up. "*Do. Not. Fire.*" Mitch tried to see where the shot had come from.

"What do you want?" The response came from the tree line. "You from the bloodsucking IRS?"

"Tree line, ten o'clock," Greg said softly.

"No." Mitch let his eyes slide to where Greg indicated. "I'm a doctor. From Eldon. I just have a few questions."

He saw then the shape just behind a tree trunk, the barrel of the rifle still pointed loosely in their direction. It slowly lowered some more.

"Show me some ID." The man half-stepped out but cradled the gun in his arms.

Mitch took out his wallet and tossed it over. "Medical ID is in the slot."

Greg did the same. The man picked them up and kept his eyes on the men. "You boys don't look like doctors. More like cops."

"Nope, check the ID," Greg replied. "We just need your help or advice on something. Something we think you might be able to help with."

The man stepped out a little more, and Mitch was finally able to see him clearly—he had white hair past his shoulders, faded jeans, and a stained chambray shirt. Though he was slim, and stood no more than 5'9, his forearms and hands were large and strong—cutting firewood would do that to you.

"Johnson Nightbird, we presume?" Mitch said.

"That's me." He checked the ID and lowered his gun. "ID could be faked, but what the hell. I ain't no conspiracy nut."

He walked up onto the deck and placed his gun by the door. Mitch and Greg followed, and he handed back their wallets.

"Nice to meet you, Mr. Nightbird." Mitch held out the cigarettes. "These are for you."

Johnson looked at them. "Where's my firewater?" His eyebrows rose. "Or my blankets?"

Mitch just stared.

"Could you be any more patronizing, you pair of white-eyed devils?" The man glared.

Mitch shook his head. "I, I, just…"

Nightbird snatched the cigarettes. "I'm only shitting you—I love Marlboro." He turned to Greg. "What did you bring me?"

Greg held his hands wide. "Goodwill and a nice smile."

"In that case, I might still shoot you." Nightbird winked. "Come on, let's grab a beer and sit a while." He turned. "Beer is three bucks a bottle."

Mitch laughed. "You got a deal. And my buddy will pay."

The trio sat on the front deck, Mitch next to Nightbird and Greg on the floor decking with his back to the wall. In the distance, they could just hear water cascading somewhere and guessed it must have been the Red Rock Canyon River.

"Peaceful," Greg said.

"That's why I like it here. Makes me humble," Nightbird replied. "When you have very little, these little things are the big things." He eyed the pair. "You guys say you were doctors?"

Mitch nodded. "I'm a general practitioner, and Greg's a medical research guy."

"Our doctor is on a fly-in, fly-out basis." Nightbird's mouth turned down. "I'm on the Otoe head council for the city. And fix cars in my spare time." He nodded to the least rusty-looking wreck. "Working on that one now."

"Good work," Mitch replied.

"Yeah, right." Nightbird winked and toasted Greg and Mitch who also sipped their beer. "Well, why did you boys drive all the way out to see an old injun?"

Mitch lowered the bottle. "You were there in Eldon in '77…during the outbreak," Mitch said.

Nightbird nodded slowly. "Yep."

"And also assisted the museum for its display on the Eldon Angels?" Greg added.

"Always happy to help." Nightbird watched them.

Mitch could tell now he was avoiding giving away anything until they showed their hands first. *They had nothing to lose*, Mitch thought. "It's happening again."

Nightbird lowered his beer. "Of course it is," he said softly while staring straight ahead.

"It's the mine water, isn't it?" Mitch asked.

Nightbird bobbed his head from side to side with his mouth turned down. "That's the end result. Not really the cause. I told them nearly 50 years ago to close that mine. All they did was fence it off." He turned to the pair. "I'm betting the fencing has come down, *huh*?"

"Yeah, and now we are getting all sorts of infections—rashes—and after we did some analysis found that it might be corrupting the mammalian genome," Greg said.

Nightbird shrugged. "I don't know what that means, but I do know that people should be kept as far from that mine as possible. Especially when it has welled up." He turned. "Hey, tell me, has there been any tremors lately?"

"Yeah, a mild one a few weeks back," Mitch replied. "Does that have something to do with it?"

Nightbird grunted. "It is in the legend."

"Of the tree god?" Mitch replied.

"*Adotte Sakima*." The old man turned slowly to him. "What do you know about it?"

Greg quickly called up some of the images of the petrified people from the CDC's files and handed it to the Native American.

"Just like the group in the museum, but these poor souls were alive in the seventies," he said.

Nightbird looked at them and then sighed. "Now they too are forever servants of the Tree God." He handed the phone back.

"Tell us about the legend." Mitch sat forward. "Everything you know."

"Everything I know." He snorted softly.

Nightbird tilted his beer back and drank half the bottle. He lowered it and stared out over his property.

Mitch thought he was about to ignore them, but after a soft burp, he began to speak as if in a trance.

"In the time before the beginning of time, before mankind was born into this great land, and maybe before any animals set foot here, there was just the water." He closed his eyes and lifted his chin as he spoke.

"A great island floated in an ocean as vast as the eye could see. It was attached by four thick ropes reaching up to the sky, which was made of rock then. There was no sun or stars and because everything was dark; there was no need for eyes. One day, a water beetle named Dayuni'si volunteered to explore underwater and found mud there that he brought back to the surface. He eventually brought up enough to make an island. He liked what he had done so he continued his work until he had brought so much mud to the surface that he created the Earth. As the Earth hardened, they pulled a sun out from behind the rock and made a rainbow.

"The first creatures who moved on their bellies could not at first see so the Great Spirit gave them eyes and then told them to stay awake for seven days and nights, but most of them could not do this.

"However, the plants that stayed awake were able to stay green all year, and the forest grew mighty. But there was no sound of voices raised in anger, or war, or even love. There were no cities, no tribes, no kingdoms. But there was a god.

"The great forests now covered the land from one side of the country to the other. And from that great early forest, there was one who rose up—not man or animal or fish, but something far older with an intelligence as old as time itself.

"It watched with its eternal eyes the changing of time. It saw the animals turn from scale to fur, and then watched as they rose up on two legs. It approved, because it needed them all. This great god as old as time needed its servants."

"*Adotte Sakima*," Greg said.

Nightbird nodded but didn't open his eyes. "But at first the tree god cared not about its servants. They were impure and needed to be changed. So, it did that. Changed them.

"But the great spirit was not happy with the tree god changing what it had created. So, he banished the *Adotte*

Sakima."

"Where? Where was it banished to?" Mitch asked. "In the mine?"

"It is everywhere." Nightbird finally opened his eyes. "These remnants of the servants that have been found are all over the country."

"So, there could be more than one of them?" Mitch asked.

"Or maybe just one but some sort of giant," Greg added. "There's something called a honey fungus that measured two and a half miles across up in the Blue Mountains in Oregon. It's thought to be the largest living organism on Earth. Maybe it's like this."

"Maybe there was many, and maybe there is only one. But even one is too many," Nightbird said. "*The Adotte Sakima is not a benign god.*"

"Well god or not, there's something weird in that water," Mitch replied. "I did a search on some microscopic flora I found in the sample I took, and it linked to something very ancient. The Museum at the University of Zürich had found plant spores that dated back a quarter of a billion years—they were a perfect match."

"It's that old? Impossible." Greg shook his head.

"That's nothing," Mitch replied. "There was a microscopic seed in the water sample that seemed to match with some of the first seed-bearing plants dating back to the Devonian Period—*400 million years ago.*"

"Primordial," Greg scoffed. "What's it doing here? Now?"

"*Adotte Sakima* does not live by our rules of lifespans of living or dying," Nightbird scoffed. "Anyway, like I said, finally the great spirit had enough of this upstart god and banished it from the land." Nightbird turned. "Banished, but not vanquished."

The old man lapsed into silence.

"*Whoa.*" Greg nodded. "That's some legend."

Nightbird snorted. "And if it was just a legend, you two wouldn't be here, right?"

Mitch and Greg looked at each other, knowing he was right.

"So?" The old Native American turned to Mitch.

"So, what happened last time? How did you stop it?" he asked. "I know that the CDC took many of the infected people away, but how did they stop more infected people turning up in the community? What did they do?"

"They didn't do anything, but you want me to tell you what happened?" Nightbird lifted his chin.

"Sure, we need to know," Greg replied. "You were the guy on the ground back then."

"They didn't do anything because they didn't have to do anything." He chuckled. "The old Otoe in me says that *Adotte Sakima* was sated, and maybe had enough servants, and enough meat in his larder, to last him a while. So, the curse of the tree god was lifted." He nodded. "That would fit with the legend."

"And what would the modern Otoe say, the one who fixes cars and sits on the council?" Mitch asked.

"He'd say the mine dried up, and then so did the curse." Nightbird turned to look at both men.

Mitch nodded. "It all comes back to the mine."

"Maybe not just the mine," Nightbird said. "That's just its highway. Something down there—maybe it's a tree god, and maybe it's something else entirely. But one thing I know—wherever that water comes from is a bad place."

Greg exhaled. "Just great. Every pothole, every crevice, or cave is a potential contamination transmission site."

"It'd be a good start though," Nightbird responded. "I told them to close the mine back in the seventies. But the powers that be decided that if there ever was demand for limestone, then a mine that was pre-dug was too valuable to destroy. Money won out."

Mitch nodded. "So, they just put a fence around it and hung a few warning signs."

Nightbird started to laugh corrosively. "Yeah, you guys love the almighty dollar. Always comes first."

"That's not fair," Mitch replied.

"Fair?" Nightbird scoffed. "You're talking to an old guy sitting on a reservation…on a postage stamp of land when all of it belonged to us in the past."

Mitch rubbed hands up through his hair and sighed. "Didn't come here for the politics, Mr. Nightbird, I came here for help to save people's lives. Adults and kids' lives."

Nightbird nodded for a moment with his mouth turned down. "You seem like good people, so I'll tell you a secret: the town leader erected a fence, but before they did, I performed a barrier ceremony." He looked up into their faces. "Make no mistake, when I said this thing was a curse, I meant it. Science alone is not the answer here."

Mitch bobbed his head, not really believing him. He faced the old man. "Is there anything else you can tell us?"

The Native American turned and saw the skepticism on Mitch's face. "Don't always trust your science, city boy." He seemed to think for a moment. "And yeah, one last thing—stay the hell out of the mine if you know what's good for you."

"But you just got through telling us that's the source of all our problems." Greg's eyes narrowed. "What's really down there?"

"I don't know. I've never been deep down there and never will. But whether it's *Adotte Sakima* or just a pool of bad water, I think you should stay a mile away." Nightbird drained his beer. "Those statues of petrified people…when I was young, I asked the elders for advice about them. They told me that some of the servants of *Adotte* who refused to serve are immediately turned to stone. And the others are altered to be more in the image of their god."

Greg half-turned to his friend. "They were transforming—remember my DNA analysis?"

"Yep." Mitch nodded.

"Did you cut yours open?" Nightbird asked.

"I don't know whether they did or not," Greg replied.

"The team here did an autopsy back in the day. Guess what they found inside some of those changed kids? I'll tell you—bones, flesh, and some of it human flesh." Nightbird shrugged. "I'm betting I know what it took to be a faithful servant of the tree god."

"Cannibalism." Greg looked away.

"A freaking nightmare." Mitch leaned his head back against the wood.

"But it stops when the mine pond drains? That's what happened last time, right?" Greg asked.

"As far as I can remember, it was about then, give or take," Nightbird replied.

"So, the strategy seems to be to keep people away from the mine when it has water in it. We lobby the town council to close the mine, permanently—by public health order. We get them to brick it up." Mitch turned to Greg. "That should keep the town safe. Then, if the mine can't flood to the surface, there'll be no contamination."

"And if there are other areas where it wells up?" Nightbird raised one silver eyebrow.

"We close them off as well. Maybe we bring in a geologist to advise us," Mitch added. "I'm pretty sure they can do some sort of underground scanning to map the limestone cave network these days? We locate all the entrances and we close 'em one at a time. We stop the infection rate in its tracks."

Greg nodded. "Sounds like a plan."

Nightbird chuckled. "I feel I'm right back in the seventies listening to those fat cats on the council board." He stood. "Well, you sharp-shooters don't need me. You guys have got this under control. Just like last time."

"What's the problem?" Greg asked.

"You forgot the curse. You can seal the mine, or just wait it out. But it'll come back. It'll find a way." Nightbird meshed his fingers and rested them on his stomach. "It always does."

"Well, would you like to make any suggestions?" Mitch forced a smile.

"I could probably lift the curse. Maybe. But it would have to be on a consultancy basis." Nightbird half-smiled.

Greg grinned. "Here it comes."

"Okay, I'll bite—how much consultancy?" Mitch asked.

"Five hundred per day." The Native American's lined face was deadpan.

"Can't afford that," Mitch said. "I'm not representing the town council, I'm just the local doctor trying to help."

"Make it 300, then." Nightbird turned to him.

"This is not a negotiation session. I just can't afford it, full stop," Mitch scoffed. "And I definitely can't afford to pay you to perform some sort of spiritual cleansing ceremony, when I think it's science that is the answer."

"Cleansing ceremony was extra. I was proposing a barrier ceremony." Nightbird laughed softly. "I can tell you gentlemen aren't ready to believe just yet. But you will be soon." He stood and used a hand to dust his old jeans off. "So, you just keep kicking the can down the road. And pray you don't hit a wall."

Mitch also got to his feet. "Thank you for talking to us." Mitch stepped off the porch. "Good luck with everything."

"And all luck and goodwill to you and Eldon. You'll need it." Nightbird nodded once and then went into his small house.

Greg followed Mitch off the deck. "How's the confidence level now?"

"On a scale of one to ten?" Mitch grinned. "About a two."

"Two?" Greg laughed. "I love an optimist."

PART 3 – RISE OF THE OLD GOD

CHAPTER 24

Eldon Sparkling Mineral Water Company, Eldon

"*Shut the fuck up*." Harry Reith glared at the dog.

The small mound of perfumed hair with the pink bow on its head was going bananas and hadn't stopped its yapping for half an hour.

"I can't friggen think straight—what's the matter with you?" Harry dipped his hand into the bag of Fancy Boy treats and dropped a bright red bone-shaped biscuit onto the carpet.

Pompom sniffed at it, then looked up at him with those tiny, black, button eyes and backed away from it. And then the yapping started again.

Harry Reith groaned and scratched his arm. It was itchy as hell, same as his back. He rolled his sleeve up and saw the rash; it was an odd pebbly thing, more brown than angry red. Trailing his fingers over it, it felt hard to the touch, like he had spilled something on himself.

He grimaced as a bolt of pain ran through his head, and for a moment, he thought he could hear music, or a lullaby, but coming from inside his head, not outside of it.

As a final insult to his body, his throat also felt like it was full of dry thorns and he grabbed the open bottle of his Eldon Spring Water—Super Health Tonic. He drank it down, and it at least calmed the prickly fire in his throat.

He winced as his stomach grumbled. Jesus, he was hungry, again, and all the time now. But lately, the snacks he had been having just didn't seem to fill him up or were never what his stomach really wanted.

He looked at the bag of Fancy Boy treats and leaned closer to read the small print—high protein and made from real beef extract. He dipped his hand in and drew out a biscuit in the shape of a cat. He sniffed it and then tossed it into his mouth. It was dry and tasted like old bone marrow. But still not what he really wanted.

Harry grimaced as Pompom's mad barking drew his head around. He stared at the dog for several minutes. As Harry stared trance-like, his mouth began to water and his stomach growled loudly as if agreeing with what he was thinking.

He carefully dipped one hand into the bag of biscuits, grabbing several, and then got down on his knees to hold out the handful of treats.

"Come on, Pompom. I've got something for you." Harry Reith licked his lips as the dog approached.

CHAPTER 25

On their return, Mitch showed Greg into his practicing rooms with Shelly in close pursuit. He'd introduced her to him, and it seemed she had a new favorite almost immediately.

Mitch went to shut the door but Shelly held onto it, sticking her head around inside.

"Can I do anything for you? Pretty quiet out here." She raised her eyebrows.

"Just coffee, large, and hold all appointments this morning," Mitch replied.

"Okay." Her eyes went to Greg. "Sugar?"

"It's Greg, actually." He grinned.

Mitch groaned as Shelly giggled.

Greg shook his head. "Just black."

Shelly crinkled her nose at him and withdrew.

Mitch waited for the door to close and then turned to his friend. "Finished?"

Greg waggled his eyebrows. "I've still got it."

"Okay, Romeo, suit up and come this way. I want to show you something." Mitch led him into the second room with the single, long cadaver refrigerator. The pair put on hospital-grade smocks and gloves, as well as paper masks. He then opened the solid steel door, pulled the table out, and flipped back the sheet revealing Buford, Harlen Bimford's hound.

"Holy shit." Greg's eyes widened above his mask.

"Was a dog once," Mitch said. He picked up a surgical probe and indicted the wound. "You can see inside that even the organs had begun to, I don't know, petrify." He looked across at his friend. "Or transition, as you suggested."

"So, this is what happens at the macro and cellular level." Greg leaned closer, then reached up to turn on a lamp that shone down into the ragged gunshot wound.

He took the probe from Mitch and began to examine the organs that Mitch hadn't yet removed during the autopsy. "It's impossible. There is no contagion, bacteria, virus, fungus, or anything I know that would generate organic changes on this level."

"Or so rapidly," Mitch replied. "It doesn't make sense on any medical or biological level."

Greg looked up, his brows raised, and Mitch held up a hand. "Don't you say it…"

"Curse." Greg grinned. "Maybe it *is*. And we should keep an open mind."

"No, this is not the dark ages," Mitch chuckled. "We've got enough weirdness going on without leaning in to the mystical."

"Really?" Greg looked back down into the dog's open chest. "Ever hear of Chief Tecumseh?"

"Nope." Mitch leaned closer as Greg moved aside the dog's heart that was like a lump of teak. "But I got a feeling I'm about to."

"Yep, Tecumseh was a Native American leader who cursed William Henry Harrison after Harrison's troops emerged victorious at the Battle of Tippecanoe. Ever since Harrison became president in 1840, every person elected to the office in 20-year intervals has died while serving as president." He turned to Mitch. "Harrison died of pneumonia after just one month in office. Abraham Lincoln, elected in 1860, was assassinated, as were James A. Garfield, 1880, and William McKinley, 1900. Both Warren G. Harding, 1920, and Franklin D. Roosevelt, 1940, died of natural causes in office, while John F. Kennedy, 1960, was assassinated. But Ronald Reagan, *elected* in 1980 and who was the target of an assassin's bullet in 1981, survived. Some say it was that missed event that finally broke the curse. And the spirit of Tecumseh was finally avenged."

"Well, someone has been doing their homework." Mitch reached up to turn the light to shine it on Greg's face.

Greg shrugged. "I know stuff." He pointed the light back down.

"It's not helping," Mitch replied. "And please don't mention Tutankhamun's tomb and the *death comes-on-swift-wings* curse."

"Damn, that was next." Greg straightened and put the probe down. "This thing should not have been living. But you said the sheriff shot it."

"Not the sheriff—Harlen Bimford, the owner. It was his faithful ole hound, Buford. Somehow, it was transformed into this and attacked him, who it loved. And was very much alive." Mitch backed up a step and took his mask off.

"Can't imagine how it functioned. And we have no idea how it got infected," Greg replied.

"I think I do. In its gut, I found trace samples of the mine's water flora. He must have drunk some. Or maybe he swam in the water up at the mine and ingested some or it was absorbed through his skin. That's all I can think of," Mitch replied. "Dump your scrubs here. Got something else to show any doubting Thomas on whether this thing was alive when it was shot."

Greg did as asked then Mitch led the military researcher into the next room and headed to a large square covered over with a blanket.

"I give you Willard." Mitch pulled the blanket away and watched Greg's face for a reaction.

Greg stared for a moment and then his eyes flicked to Mitch. "And?"

Mitch turned to look into the cage—it was empty, and the bars were pulled in, making a hole in one corner.

"Is it invisible?" Greg asked.

"No, but it's damned gone." He cursed again as he threw the blanket down on top of the cage. "I fed a rat I caught some of the mine water and it began to change within a few hours. It was becoming just like the dog."

"The faithful old dog that attacked its owner?" Greg raised his eyebrows.

"Shelly?" Mitch called.

She appeared, looked around, and pointed to the two coffees that had been waiting for them. Her brows came together. "It's probably cold now. Want some more?"

Mitch shook his head and then pointed at the cage. "Did you come in here? There was a laboratory rat in this cage, and it seems to have got out."

"No, I didn't. But if I saw that huge rat that had been hanging around, I'm more than likely to drop a heavy book on it." She made a gagging expression.

"This one, stay away from," Greg said.

"Okay, thanks, Shelly. Keep a lookout and tell me if you see it. But don't go near it." Mitch sighed.

She nodded and went outside.

"There goes my controled experiment." He blew air between his lips.

"One question," Greg said. "Has anyone checked on Mr. Bimford lately? You know, the guy attacked by his friendly old dog that was turning to something like wood?"

"I'm thinking that should be our next stop," Mitch replied. "But first, it's time to visit the mayor and see if we can get some help."

CHAPTER 26

Mitch drove Greg up the familiar private road toward the line of orange trees. Peeking above them was the three-story Georgian mansion with huge white columns framing a double door entrance, ivy climbing all the way up one wall, and box hedges creating borders around smaller gardens.

"Very nice. I could live here," Greg said. "When are you going to run for mayor?"

"*Pfft*. All that money, respect, and luxury? Way too rich for my blood." Mitch grinned. "I'm happy being one of the little guys."

"Nah, you were always a leader, not a follower," Greg added. "You'd be good at it. Give it a run after you've added a few years."

"And a few pounds." Mitch grinned. "Wait until you meet Mayor Melnick."

They pulled up out front and stepped out of the car. Mitch thought it seemed like the property was even bigger without the party crowd. Also, quieter.

Mitch turned at the top of the steps. "And remember, they're not called butlers or maids, they're called staff."

"Got it—to their face." Greg snorted. "Because I'd still be telling everyone I had a butler, not staff."

Mitch pressed the bell and within seconds, one of the huge doors was pulled inward.

A middle-aged man in a perfectly pressed suit Mitch had seen serving drinks at the mayor's cookout stood rod straight in the doorway.

"Doctor Taylor, how can I help you?" He reserved a flat smile for Mitch, but his eyes shot Greg a cool gaze as they lingered on him for a moment or two.

"Good morning, Alston," Mitch began. "Please tell the mayor I'd like a brief word about the work we're doing regarding Hank and Alfie."

His eyes went to Greg again and the suspicion was still writ large on his face. "And who else should I say is calling?"

"Doctor Taylor and associate." Mitch stared back, not giving an inch.

"Very good, Doctor Taylor." He closed the door on them.

Greg chuckled. "He seems nice."

A few minutes later, Keith Melnick appeared in a polo shirt and pressed pants.

He greeted Mitch warmly and then stood back. "And who have we here?"

Greg stuck his hand out. "Good morning, Mayor Melnick. I'm a friend of Mitch's and also work in the medical field."

"Private research or corporate?" Melnick held onto his hand, searching his face.

"Neither actually—military," Greg replied.

Melnick dropped his hand and his eyes slid back to Mitch.

Mitch patted Greg's shoulder. "He's a medically experienced friend acting in a private capacity as a sounding board. But it *is* why we're here. We need a little more help. This thing that infected Hank and Alfie…"

"You found Alfie?" Melnick asked.

"No, but—" Mitch began.

"So, we still don't know it infected Alfie, if at all, then?" Melnick's brows rose.

The guy was a bulldozer and Mitch knew then how this was going to go. "Mayor, whatever is affecting people in this town…"

"Which people? The sheriff told me about Harlen's dog, Buford I think he said. But who else?" The mayor's smile was stuck on and held no warmth.

"Mayor, we have missing people, and we know it was caused by whatever it is leaking out of the mine. I conducted a test on a rat, and it changed into something…*unnatural*. We need to bring in some professional help on this one." Mitch's jaws clenched.

Melnick frowned. "You have this *changed* rat? I want to see it."

"Not anymore. It escaped." Mitch knew how feeble that sounded, and by the look on Melnick's face, he did too.

Melnick turned to Greg. "Did you see it?"

Greg shook his head. "I didn't need to, I saw the DNA evidence, and there was definitely a biological agent that acted as an accelerant for genome changes at the DNA level."

"I see." Melnick nodded as he walked a few paces further out onto his front porch, leaving the door open behind him.

He turned. "So, we have a dead man, that the sheriff is thinking is a potential homicide case. We have a dead dog, that I believe was diseased, rabies maybe. We have a deformed rat, missing. And we have…what else?"

Mitch felt his face going red as his temples throbbed.

Melnick reached out and put an arm over his shoulders. "Mitch, I trust your judgment. And my request still stands for you to handle this with the sheriff, as he is one of the most competent men in the town."

He stopped, glanced at Greg, and then back to Mitch. "If things start to get a little more complicated, then we can revisit the discussion on whether we need more resources." He looked at Mitch from under lowered brows. "But you know my reservations on that. Eldon survives on tourist income, and anything we do to jeopardize that could spell disaster for working families in and all around the town and country."

Mitch sighed. "I think we have a bigger problem than you imagine."

"I can only *imagine* based on the facts presented to me. Until I see something more compelling, then I can't imagine authorizing anything more." Melnick waited a moment as he stared back at Mitch. "I think we're done here, Doctor Taylor." He reached down to take Mitch's hand and shook it. "Keep up the good work—I like you, I really do. And let me tell you, I appreciate your passion and all your hard work."

Melnick turned to Greg and simply nodded. "And now, I have work to do."

The mayor vanished back inside, and then Alston closed the door without a single glance at either of them.

Greg turned. "We sure showed him."

"Yep, had him eating out of my hand." Mitch chuckled. "Now do you see what I'm up against?"

"Yeah. But you and I both know something weird is going on. And I'm hoping that by the time we *do* collect enough proof, it isn't too late."

Mitch nodded. "Then only one thing to do: gather more proof. Let's pay a visit to dear old Mr. Harlen Bimford."

*****

Mitch drove slowly past Harlen's drug and convenience store, noticing that the door usually open and welcoming was now shut up tight.

"He never shuts that door this time of day." Mitch slowed to a crawl.

"Maybe he's in mourning for his dog," Greg said.

"Yeah, maybe." Mitch pulled into the sidewalk and pushed his door open. He put his hand over his eyes from the midday sunshine and squinted at the store.

"And all dark inside," he observed.

The pair approached the door and cupped their hands around their eyes to peer inside.

"Nothing," Greg replied slowly. He shifted his gaze. "But I can see a few things scattered on the floor."

"Sheriff said he was attacked by Buford, so maybe he just hasn't got around to cleaning up yet." Mitch moved to the door.

"Was he hurt?" Greg turned to him.

"Kehoe didn't mention it. Otherwise, ole Harlen might have paid me a visit. Come on." He tried the door but it wouldn't budge. "Locked."

"'Round back?" Greg turned to the corner. "Try this way."

Mitch followed down the sidewalk and then took a hard right past a pottery shop. He turned about and saw that the street was unnaturally quiet. Odd, given it was a Thursday, and it was neither overly hot nor cold.

The rear of the shops was a laneway with a few trashcans out, some garages or vans parked, and power poles. The pair quickly made their way to the back of Harlen's shop.

"This looks like it," Mitch said.

Greg lifted the shop's trashcan's lid and peered in. "He likes his soda." He reached in and pulled an empty bottle out. "Eldon Spring Water—Super Health Tonic." He was about to close it and then paused. He turned about, reached for a broken length of rod, and used it to lift something else from the bin's interior.

He held it out. "Torn shirt, with blood." He looked up. "The dog's blood or owner's?"

Mitch frowned. "Ripped to shreds. But then again, that dog thing had teeth like rose thorns. Good reason to check on the guy." He turned to the door. "Here goes." He knocked on the door, hard.

They waited a few moments, while Mitch held his ear closer.

"Nothing." He tried the door handle and found it locked.

"He might be out," Greg said.

"Where? The guy is about 75 in the shade." Mitch grinned. "I really hope he's not sitting in my office waiting room bleeding out."

"We should call the sheriff. I mean, this is his territory," Greg said.

"No, we can't wait for him. Harlen could be hurt or worse." Mitch listened at the door again. "Gotta go in—no one left behind to suffer."

"Geez, you still hung up on that?" Greg scoffed. "Let it go, Mitch. Sheriff can be here in a minute or two. Come on, buddy, drop that Syrian baggage."

Mitch frowned. "I'm not hung up on anything."

"It wasn't your fault," Greg replied evenly.

"Listen, I…" Mitch put his hands on his hips and stared at the ground for a moment. He didn't come here just to walk away. Besides, if someone was hurt, he was never walking away again.

Maybe I am hung up, he thought.

He decided. "Fuck it. Potential medical emergency, we're going in."

He grabbed the handle, leaned back a little, and then rammed his shoulder into the door. It gave off a sound of wood cracking but didn't budge.

"One more." He held onto the door handle but leaned back about an arm's length this time and then pulled and propelled himself into the door. It exploded inward with a shower of splintered wood.

The pair went in fast, Mitch going left and Greg right, and found themselves in the rear of Harlen's shop, which he had obviously been using as a kitchen, washroom, and storeroom.

Greg put his arm over his lower face. "Jesus, spoiled food."

"Spoiled something," Mitch replied.

He tried the light switch and got nothing. "Of course they won't work."

"Got a flashlight?" Greg asked.

"Yeah, in my car." Mitch pushed the door open a little further to give them some more light and also some better quality air.

"You're off the hook." Greg found a flashlight on a shelf. He switched it on, and though the beam was a little yellow, it would do the job in the darkness.

Mitch held up a hand. "Mr. Bimford? Harlen? It's Doctor Taylor. I took over from Ben Wainright." He tilted his head to listen but heard nothing.

"Time to advance, buddy," Greg said softly.

"Lead on," Mitch said.

Greg lifted the flashlight and paused to speak over his shoulder. "Why do I wish I had a sidearm right now?"

"Stay cool, eyes out," Mitch whispered.

Greg headed in, moving the beam of light from one side of the passageway to the other as he went. "Got a room here." He stopped and then quickly stuck his head around with the light. "Clear."

The next room had a disheveled bed pushed into a corner so it seemed old Harlen was sleeping in the back of his shop. The room was filthy, with the sheets yellow and rumpled, and dog food tins and empty meat packets scattered about.

"He was eating dog food?" Greg asked.

"Protein," Mitch replied, suddenly remembering the state of Hank Bell after Alfie had finished with him. "We might have a problem here."

The pair moved at near glacial speed and with a silence only learned from Special Forces duty. Mitch felt himself moving into a hyper-alert state just like when on-mission.

They paused at the doorway to the large area at the front of the shop. Light from the glass windows gave them some illumination but with the lights out there were still far too many shadows.

Mitch held up a hand to his friend and stepped just inside the doorway. "Mr. Bimford? It's Doctor Taylor, are you there?"

They waited for a response, but the only sound was the soft

hum of a refrigerator against a far wall.

Greg looked to Mitch and nodded, and both men went into the room, Mitch to the left and Greg to the right. The pair searched the aisles of the shop until Greg called out.

"Got him. Over here."

Mitch followed the flashlight beam and rounded a line of shelves. It was Harlen, probably. The man was slumped in a chair, empty soda bottles surrounding him, and a shotgun between his knees. The top of his head was missing.

"Ah, shit." Mitch grimaced. "Poor guy."

"Guess the old fella's dog dying was too much to bear." Greg held the light closer. "Hey, come here and look at this."

Mitch leaned closer. The top of the skull from the nose upward was missing, and the ceiling above was spattered with a dry, brown crusting. But there was little blood. Or at least little liquid blood or glutinous cranial matter.

Greg held the light into the cavity. "It's dry. Like he was a year-old corpse." He moved the flashlight.

Mitch carefully reached out to pull Harlen's shirt aside and saw the rash. He immediately let it go and looked around, found a wooden spoon on the shelf, and used it to hold the shirt aside.

"That's no ordinary rash," he observed. "A little like one of the town kids had on his lower back, but much more advanced."

Greg lifted his sleeve and saw the rash became more like dark scaling. He looked up. "Like his dog?"

"I want to examine him. If this skin condition was transmitted from the dog to Harlen through a bite, then just staying away from the mine might not be enough." Mitch let the man's collar drop. "Might be the evidence I need to convince Mayor Melnick to call in the cavalry."

"Okay, so what now? Putting my biomedical hat on, I'm going to suggest it's not a good idea to stick this guy in your car. Or us even to be handling him without at least gloves and masks." Greg straightened.

"Yeah, I'll give Sheriff Kehoe a call and then arrange for Harlen to be brought into my rooms for analysis." Mitch turned about. "Let's get out of here and get some fresh air."

CHAPTER 27

Back at Mitch's practice rooms, Harlen Bimford's naked body was stretched out on the steel operating table. Greg had acted as the forensic technician and had undressed the man and cleaned his body.

Sheriff Kehoe stood back against the wall with a mask over his mouth and nose and a drained-looking complexion.

Mitch walked once around the body, his training as a physician taking over now. He had been involved in autopsies before and he had two options for approaching his task: the first, the forensic autopsy, was used to determine the cause, mode, and manner of death. But given the top half of the man's head was blown off by his own hand, that immediately became redundant.

However, the second option, a clinical autopsy, that also involved a human dissection of the abdominal and thoracic regions, delivered more insight into pathological processes and determined what factors contributed to a patient's death. For example, biological material for infectious disease testing can be collected during an autopsy, and this would be critical for understanding and preparing for any future cases of this thing he had come to know as Angel Syndrome.

"Let's begin." His first step was the external examination, and Mitch spoke in a methodical and emotionless tone as he looked over Harlen's body.

"Obvious manifestation of significant skin trauma caused by immune system response to some sort of allergen, toxin, or microbial intrusion to the system."

He ran a hand over the arm and then lifted it by the wrist. There was a pebbly rash starting from the hand, but as it worked its way up the arm, the lumps got bigger, and then sharper, until they became like thorns at the upper bicep.

"Thickening of the derma by what seems like keratin, but

isn't."

He then noted the chest that had developed a hard, scaled texture that ran from the neck down to the pubis. Mitch knocked on it, making a hard shell-like noise. "Epidermal layers are crusted to the point of creating a bark-like…growth."

"Scleroderma?" Greg asked.

"Sclero-what?" Kehoe asked.

"Scleroderma." Mitch nodded. "Or possibly some sort of variation." He looked up at the sheriff. "It's a rare skin disease that involves the hardening and tightening of the skin and connective tissues. But it usually affects women more often than men and is also site-specific, not over the entire body—it usually targets the joints, knuckles, and looks more like angry callouses. But old Harlen here is beginning to look more like a spiked tortoise."

"Never seen or heard of anything like this before," Kehoe muttered.

Mitch looked up at the sheriff. "I have, in Ben Wainright's notes."

"Or on Harlen's dog," Greg added.

Mitch nodded. "That reminds me." He checked the man's arm and quickly found the bite. It seemed to have been healing nicely and there was no sign of infection surrounding the wound.

"From looking at this, not sure if the dog transmitted the infection. Maybe it went straight to his bloodstream without causing any epidermal reaction." He moved to the top of the body. "Okay, hold onto your lunch, kids, I'm going in."

Mitch then began the internal examination. Greg had already placed a *head block* under the neck and shoulders of the old man. Its role was to hyperflex the neck, making the spine arch backward while stretching and pushing the chest upward to make it easier to incise.

Mitch began and didn't use a standard Y-shaped incision, but instead a double T-shape with the first a line across the shoulder blades, then running down the front of the chest, continuing around and to just below the belly button. Then, another horizontal incision was made from one side of the lower belly to the other.

Expectedly, bleeding was non-existent because the pull of

gravity is exerting the only blood pressure at this point, as there is a complete lack of cardiac functionality.

Greg helped Mitch pull the skin back to fully expose the ribs and sternum, and then used bone-shear clips to cut through each of the ribs so he could then lift the frontal ribs and sternum away like a large, grisly plate to expose the internal organs.

Mitch handed the rib plate to Greg who set it aside.

"*Hooo-ley* crap." Mitch peered into the cavity.

"How was this guy even alive?" Greg asked.

Mitch blew air between his lips. "Maybe it happened post mort." He grimaced behind his mask. "Okay." He reached in.

The lungs, heart, and stomach were all a brown or black, but not so much from the corruption of the flesh and blood; instead, they had a grainy texture. Also running over everything were veins or webbing that looked like the spidery roots you find when you dig up a small tree.

"I'm betting Harlen would have had similar alterations in his head before he blew it off," Greg said.

Mitch cut free the stomach, and rather than being its usual elastic grey-purple bag, it was now brown, hard, and more like a leather satchel. He set it on a lab tray and sliced it open.

Mitch hated this part of an autopsy and held his breath in anticipation—stomachs always had a mix of digested and undigested food, depending on how healthy the individual was. And inside Harlen were lumps of dog food, raw meat, and even a single mouse, still covered in fur.

"He ate a mouse?" Kehoe grimaced.

"Yeah, definitely carnivore," Greg replied.

Mitch extracted some of the liquid into a test tube and stood it in a rack. He also cut away a few pieces of flesh from different organs and also from within the chest cavity, which he sealed in individual jars. He handed each to Greg who wrote their name and time of extraction on each.

"Just like with his dog, I'm betting we find the same sort of active influencing agent that is reorganizing his cellular structure, as well as his DNA. It's the thing we found in the mine water." He looked up. "Somehow, Harlen was infected, just like his dog."

"From the dog," Kehoe announced.

"I don't know that," Mitch replied. "Looks to me like their

state of change was running in tandem, and not one after the other." Mitch stood back. "His entire body was undergoing a radical alteration."

"Transitioning," Greg replied. He pointed to the trays of removed organs. "Look."

"What the hell?" Kehoe craned forward.

The organs that had the whitish tendrils or spidery roots covering them were moving, and the webbing seemed to be trying to pull them all together.

"If I didn't know better, I'd say they're trying to put themselves back together," Mitch said softly.

"Pluripotent dedifferentiation," Greg whispered.

"Say again?" Mitch turned.

Greg kept his eyes on the organs as they merged within the webbing. "It's where plants regenerate tissue or even whole organelles after injury."

"I have no idea what's going on here." Mitch shook his head slowly. "And we still don't know what the biological objective is." He sighed. "I'll close this guy up later. Right now, I want a coffee, or something even stronger."

He pulled his hands from his gloves and dropped them into a bio-hazard bin, and the group placed their smocks in a laundry basket.

Outside in the fresh air, Mitch turned to the sheriff. "Sheriff, we need outside help on this. The mayor is refusing to allow me to take it to any of the external bodies for fear of creating a panic."

Kehoe nodded. "I know, and I can understand that."

Mitch stood in front of him. "We don't have an understanding or a handle on this yet. This could be cataclysmic for the town if we do nothing."

Kehoe nodded. "But the mine is closed off now. No mine, no water from the mine, no infections, right?"

"That's not enough," Greg said. "Johnson Nightfoot, who, *ah*, worked with Doctor Wainright during the first outbreak, said this will go on, and even may get worse, while the mine is flooded."

Kehoe raised his eyebrows. "Then our problem is solved. I checked on the mine this morning: the water is all gone."

CHAPTER 28

Greg and Mitch skidded to a stop at the bottom of the side road leading up to the mine. The pair stepped out, and Greg approached the seven-foot gate that barred access.

He turned. "Well, the sheriff did as you suggested."

"Yeah, he's a good man." Mitch fished in his pocket for the keys that Kehoe had given him. "I kinda get the feeling he believes us as well. And I bet quietly supports us too but just won't go on record. Yet."

Mitch unlocked the padlock and dragged the huge gate open. "We'll drive up the hill. Get out at the top."

He drove the car in and jumped out to close the gate behind them. But left it unlocked. Then they headed up the half-mile incline until they came to another gate.

"I think you're right—Kehoe definitely believes you." Greg got out, and the pair walked forward to peer through the fencing.

Mitch unlocked it and they stepped through. He left the gate open this time; for some reason, Mitch had the urge to have a fast and clear path back to the car if they needed it.

Greg threw a hand out to Mitch and grabbed his arm, stopping him. "You hear that?"

Mitch turned back and concentrated. He then did hear something. It sounded like a rattle and a low chanting. And there was also a smell, like rosemary and eucalyptus leaves burning.

He looked about at the dry trees and spindly underbrush. "Not a great place to be caught if there's a brushfire."

"Well, we're here now, so we need to check it out. And if there is a fire, we need to report it," Greg said and nodded forward. "Besides, I'm dying to see this mystical mine of yours."

They crested the steep hill and slowed. The last time Mitch

had come here, the dry and dusty mine had been converted to an oasis. Now the water had evaporated or drained away, but the banks of the dry pond were still lush and green, and the trees closest looked bountiful and healthy.

Greg walked forward and stared into the basin. It had a greenish tinge on the bottom and sides that gave off an odor like overcooked broccoli.

Greg waved a hand in front of his face. "Phew. Tide is out."

"Yeah, whatever those seeds and spores were, they're not rotting just yet." Mitch turned about. "The ground must be saturated, as the plants are still enjoying the wet."

Greg stepped into the basin, put a hand over his eyes, and squinted into the dark hole. "Can't see a thing." He walked up to the mine edge and peered in. "*Hallooo!*"

The echo bounced back several times, but that was it. He turned. "Still smells damp in there."

"Yeah, Kehoe was right. The mine pond has dried up, but it seems to still be receding."

"Back to where it came from," Greg replied. He turned to Mitch. "What do you want to do?" He shook his head. "You know what? I can still smell that weird smoke. It's even stronger here."

He turned back to the mine, just as a figure appeared out of the stygian darkness of its mouth.

"*Jesus.*" Greg fell backward.

"Not quite, but close." Nightbird laughed out loud as he stepped into the light.

"That's how assholes get themselves shot." Greg scrambled to his feet.

"What are you doing here?" Mitch demanded.

The old Native American shrugged. "Same thing you are, I guess. Checking on the state of the mine."

"I'm betting that smoke we can smell is your doing?" Mitch replied.

"Yep." Nightbird briefly turned to the mine entrance. "I performed a barrier spell. But I doubt it will hold for too long."

"Barrier spell, *huh*?" Greg scoffed. "Welcome to the dark ages."

"That's right." Nightbird glared. "And given you two *men of science* are baffled and I'm the only one that has dealt with this before, I suggest you quit the sneering and pay attention."

He went on. "This outbreak, or madness, or curse, will go on until *it* decides it is finished. It may end today, or tomorrow, in a week, or a month. The last time, nothing we did stopped it. It decided to stop itself when it was good and ready."

"*It?*" Greg turned to Mitch.

"*Adotte Sakima*, the tree god, right?" Mitch replied evenly.

"That's right." Nightbird walked further out a few paces and looked up at the sky. "Sundown is coming soon. I don't want to be around these parts in the dark."

"Why, what happens after dark?" Greg asked.

"Maybe nothing," Nightbird replied. "But look around."

Greg and Mitch did as requested. Mitch saw it then—the footprints, lots of them. Some of them barefoot.

"Many people have been up here." He frowned. "Some without shoes. And they seem to head into the mine. Not many come back out."

"They must have come out another way," Greg replied. "Or the tracks were obscured."

"What were they doing in there?" Mitch asked.

"Serving the tree god," Nightbird replied. "Like I said, if they are in there, I don't want to be here if they come out to feed. Or are looking for more food for their god." He lifted his chin. "But that's just an old superstitious injun talking, right?"

"Lighten up. We're trying to protect the community, just like you," Mitch replied.

Nightbird turned back and his expression softened. "Okay. Come on, let's get out of here. Maybe you can return the favor and buy me a beer."

"Hey, you made us pay for those beers last time," Greg scoffed.

Nightbird held his arms wide. "Part of my consultancy fee."

Mitch laughed softly and slapped his friend on the shoulder. "There's nothing else we can do here. The upside is the mine pond is draining away, so at least there should be no more Angel Syndrome cases turning up."

Greg turned back to the mine. "Barrier spell…now I've heard everything." He shook his head and followed his friend.

CHAPTER 29

Joanne and Gary Adams stood on the back porch just staring out over the grass hedge to the land beyond their property line.

Both held bottles of Eldon Spring Water—Super Health Tonic, and neither bothered checking on their son James anymore. Ever since he had returned from hanging out with his friends up at the mine, he had been sullen and then withdrawn to his room where he had pulled the blinds, eventually crawling beneath the bedcovers and staying there.

He had said, when he was still speaking to them, that he heard singing. Joanne and Gary had thought it was a hallucination brought on by a passing fever accompanied by a pebbly rash that had covered his body.

But now they heard it too.

CHAPTER 30

"The tribes had no written language." Johnson Nightbird put his beer down. "The first written language, as Europeans know it, was created by the Cherokee, in the early 1800s. It was a syllabary, because each of the graphic symbols represents a syllable."

"Always wondered about that," Greg said. "How you passed along information from one generation to the next without some form of writing."

Nightbird nodded. "Our history is one that is spoken and sung. But there were also symbols that had wide meaning across the tribes. The bear symbol meant strength; the turtle, long life and health; crossed arrows meant friendship; and so on.

"We carved these images in stone and drew them on rock faces, and our symbols for a word or a phrase have been found dating to 5,000 years ago." He leaned forward. "But the original people have been here longer than that. They most likely arrived 15,000 years ago over the land bridge to the far north."

He held up a finger and waggled it at them. "And there is also an ancient symbol that was universal among the tribes from the frozen north to the southern deserts, and it was for the 'great tree.'"

He smiled. "For years, Europeans interpreted it to mean life, or abundance, or protection. But we knew it as something different. We knew it as a warning of great danger."

"Your tree god," Greg said.

"Everyone's tree god," Mitch replied. "Whether we like it or not."

"Yeah, I'm not buying that." Greg sat back. "Everything I've seen and heard to date will have a scientific explanation, and not some legendary being or tree or entity hidden down in caves below Eldon. To me, I see an ancient contaminant or biological pathogen that is infecting people. An ancient germ leaks to the surface that we have little immunity defenses against. End of story." Greg looked to Mitch. "Frankly, Mitch, this should have gone to the CDC for their quarantine and clean-up, and the mayor can go to hell."

"I know, I know," Mitch sighed. "But this is my home now, and if it means I have to be super vigilant and watch out for more cases, I'll do that. If I saw anything significant happening again, then yeah, sure, I'll do that in a blink." He crossed his heart. "I promise."

"Well, that's good enough for me." Greg chuckled and leaned back in his seat. "So, what now?"

Mitch shrugged. "The water has receded and should be totally gone soon. We've seen or heard nothing out of the ordinary, so for now, we just watch and wait."

"Harlen wasn't out of the ordinary enough for you?" Greg raised his eyebrows. "Or the dog, or your rat?"

"I'm hoping he was the last. And I think that rat went to rat Heaven… or Hell," Mitch replied. He turned to the old Native American. "What do you think, Johnson?"

"Maybe it's over, maybe it isn't." Nightbird waved his hand to the barman and ordered some more drinks. "If it's still all quiet in 24 hours, then maybe our work here is done and I can go back home."

"Here's hoping." Mitch lifted the beer and clinked the bottle with the two other men.

Nightbird sipped and let out a long sigh of pleasure. "And if it is over, then we can all agree it was my barrier spell that did it."

"Of course it was." Greg chuckled and took a long gulp of beer. "Mitch, I'll hang out for another day, then I'll head back home as well. But I think I'll do a little more digging on those missing Eldon people from way back in the seventies. I don't mind telling you I think it's all a bit freaky, and one X-Files level mystery."

Nightbird stared into his drink. "Maybe you should leave it be."

"Too late for that now," Greg replied.

Nightbird looked at the man from under lowered brows. "You might not like what you find."

Mitch gripped his shoulder. "If you do poke around, let me

know what you find. And thanks for everything. I know it's been tough."

"Anytime." Greg grinned. "Yeah, been wild, but my pleasure."

"*Pfft*, pair of city pussies," Nightbird scoffed at the pair.

"So, we're pussies now?" Greg laughed.

The Native American put his beer down. "Mr. Greg, one bit of advice for the road: curiosity killed the cat." He winked at Greg. "The pussycat."

CHAPTER 31

Nine days later

"So, it's over?" Karen raised her coffee mug in a toast.

Mitch clinked his steaming mug against hers. "I think so. Or at least I hope so." He smiled. "No more skin rashes, abnormalities, or even psychotic kids. I would have felt better if I could have brought in some outside experts, but…" He shrugged. "Politics."

"Keith mentioned it," Karen replied. "I don't blame the mayor for trying to look out for the town's interests. I mean, yelling *contagious disease* in a small town reliant on tourism, is the same as yelling *shark* at a beach."

"Yeah, I guess." He looked out through the window at Karen's sasanqua camellia trees as the wind rustled their leaves, making them shimmer in the late afternoon sun.

He turned back, suddenly feeling relieved, and happier than he had in years. He loved Eldon, no matter the weirdness he had encountered. And he loved it here even more because he had a growing affection for Karen, and even better, he felt her for him too.

On the other side of the living room, Benji was on his knees, brows knitted as he worked on some sort of Lego model with the intensity of a nuclear scientist working with radioactive fuel rods.

Mitch turned back. "I'm just glad we managed to keep the local kids out of the mine pool when it filled up. Seems that was the source of our infection, and if it had of turned into the local swimming hole, everything might have gotten a lot worse."

Benji stopped his Lego building and half-turned. "What?"

Mitch turned back to Karen's son. "Yeah, it seems there was something in the water that made people sick." Mitch raised his eyebrows. "But it's all gone now. All leaked away."

"What do you mean by sick? Like vomiting and stuff?"

Benji fully faced him, his eyes like moons.

"Yes, and worse." He narrowed his eyes. "You didn't swim in it, did you?'

"Me, no." He looked back down at his Legos but didn't start working on it again.

"Benji, did you go up there when it was full of water?" Karen asked.

He shrugged and picked up his model.

"Benji?" she pressed.

"My friends swam in it. But I didn't." His words tumbled out fast. "Neither did Isabella."

"Okay." Mitch turned in his seat. "Who *did* go in?"

"James, he went in first, then Kenny, Gemma, and also fat Alf."

"Don't call him fat." Karen frowned. "He's just well fed."

No wonder she's in politics, Mitch thought. But alarms went off in Mitch's head at hearing the kid's name.

"Alf is Alfie Bell, Hank's son, right?" Mitch asked.

"That's right." Karen stared, hard now. "What is it?"

He held up a hand. "So, just four kids, *huh*? I remember there were a lot of footprints up there for just four of them. When did you say you went in?"

Benji thought for a moment. "Weeks and weeks back, when it was real hot. Maybe they went back there, or it was some other kids. Everyone knew the pond was full again. It was real nice."

"A few weeks back." Mitch seemed to remember seeing the kid, James, come in with a mild rash, but that was it. He turned to Benji again. "Hey, have you seen, *uh*, James, Gemma, or any of the others since?"

Benji tilted his head and his brow furrowed. "*Nah*, not for a long time."

Mitch frowned. "Not even at school?"

"It's school holidays," Karen said.

"But out of school, or anywhere?" Mitch pressed.

Benji shook his head and Mitch rubbed his chin for a moment. "Maybe I should visit them then, just to check they're okay."

"Mitch?" A deep line appeared between Karen's brows.

He shook his head. "Probably nothing."

"You need to see them," Karen pronounced.

"I could come...show you where they live," Benji pronounced.

"We should go, *now*," Karen said. "If it was Benji, I'd want him checked out, like yesterday."

"I agree, but it might panic Mom or Dad if the town doctor turns up with the vice mayor."

Karen snorted. "I know just about everyone in the town. *You're* more likely to scare them than me."

Benji shook his head. "He's not that scary, Mom." He swung to Mitch. "She can stay in the car, and we can go and see them. They all know me."

Mitch grinned. "Hey, maybe your mom and I should stay in the car so just you can examine them."

"Sure. Can I wear one of those listening things around my neck?" Benji immediately was onboard with the idea.

"It's called a stethoscope. And the only people who wear them around their neck are actors playing doctors." Mitch pushed his coffee mug back onto the table. "Okay, gang, let's go and pay some people a visit."

CHAPTER 32

Town of Jasper, Pickens County, Georgia

Greg Samson got out of his rental and stretched his back. The town was small, even smaller than Eldon, and colder, with a range of white-peaked mountains lying like slumbering leviathans just to the north.

Greg bet that on a clear and cloudless day, they'd seem like they were right in your backyard. In fact, he'd read that Jasper was nicknamed *The First Mountain City*, and he could see why.

But what brought him here was that it was just 50 miles north of Atlanta, the headquarters of the Center for Disease Control, or CDC. He doubted many people cared about that. But what wasn't too widely known, at least from the public's perspective, was it was home to one of the CDC's test and storage laboratories. It was an out-of-the-way, secluded place, where they could conduct research experiments or store the results of those experiments that might not have thrilled the locals if they knew what was going on.

His CDC contacts had given him the location of the lab after he had pressed them hard about the people taken from Eldon in 1977, and it seemed this is where they ended up.

The Jasper CDC facility wasn't used much anymore and seemed to have been mothballed. But Greg was betting that its secrets lay undisturbed, and given that the only security was an occasional drive-by from the local sheriff once or twice an evening, he knew he'd be able to take a little look-see to satisfy his, and Mitch's, curiosity.

Greg climbed back into his car and drove off the main street, heading to the outskirts of the town, and soon he came to a small and well-maintained road with a single signpost telling him to, *Keep Out – Private Property*.

Greg slowed but kept on going. It was afternoon, and he'd

been driving for many hours. He'd grab a bite in town and just hang-out until dusk, and then pay them a little visit then.

He'd been given access codes and slide keys, plus a warning—don't get caught. And if he did, to flatly refuse to tell them about where he got his information.

He grinned—he already had his story straight: blame the dead guy. He could simply say that Eldon's old Doc Wainright had a notebook that detailed what happened to the missing people. He was just following the old guy's lead.

Greg drove back into town, pulled up down the road from a burger joint, spent a few hours having the best hamburger, fries, pie, and endless coffee he'd had in years. He knew why Mitch liked Eldon; there was something about small towns that weren't as rushed, were friendlier, and much better value.

He sat staring out the window for a while. *I could live in a place like this*, he thought. He straightened. And why didn't he? Life was too short to be stuck in an office in a big city forever.

"More coffee?" the pretty waitress asked, breaking his reverie.

"Yes, please." He smiled up at her. "I like this town."

She smiled, showing a row of perfect teeth that would have been at home in a toothpaste commercial. "So do I." She held his eyes for a moment, and then headed back to the counter.

Greg watched her go. *I am definitely looking into this when I get back*, he thought resolutely.

In a blink, he folded the newspaper, checked his watch, and looked out through the large window. The sun was hitting the horizon and he wanted to check out the facility then be on the road back home within a few hours.

He paid, tipping big, and earned another wide smile from the waitress. "I'll see you again soon."

"I hope so," she said and toasted him with the coffee pot.

Greg headed back to his car, feeling good. He checked he had everything: flashlight, card keys, and codes. And finally, a flat K-bar knife. He didn't expect to need it for self-defense and if he was challenged, he'd certainly comply with any law enforcement. But the military knives had a stout blade, tanto edge, and were immensely strong. If he needed a knife, a chisel, or a jemmy, the K-bar would do wonders.

He drove up the unnamed road to the facility and then

slowed as he approached the wire fence. He had the key to the padlock and got out to unlock and push it back.

He noticed that the padlock was a little hard to turn, which for him was a good sign—no one had entered here for a while.

Greg shut the gate and hung the lock back in place without closing it, and then drove the few hundred yards to the large, flat building. He had no doubt that it extended below-ground—for covert work, best to leave a small footprint above but make use of the below-ground real estate.

Greg eased the car door open and then turned slowly. The sun was now just an orange blush on the horizon. From what he could see, inside the building were no lights, no sound, and the smell was more of the surrounding forest than of any sort of industry or human habitation.

If it wasn't for the well-kept state of the building, he'd have thought the facility was abandoned. *Maybe that was the idea*, he thought.

He ignored the large front doors, as he had been told there was a service entrance around the side, and he quickly found the smaller steel door. The code pad took his numbers, a small red light flicked to green, there was a sturdy *clunk*, and the door popped open. He took one last look around and then entered quickly, shutting the door behind him to stand with his back to it, then just listened.

Inside was darker than Hades itself, and he had no chance of his eyes adapting, so in another few seconds, he switched on his flashlight and panned it around.

He found himself in a storage room with what looked like medical supplies, toilet paper, stationery, and other odds and ends in boxes and crates. There were two doors on the far wall, and his contact had described the layout and suggested the northern door was the one he should take.

Greg went in and quickly crossed through several rooms, down corridors, and ignored an elevator to instead use the fire stairs to drop down two floors to the lower storage and containment areas.

Once again, he needed a code to enter the more fortified area of the facility and eased in to shine his light down a long and wide corridor—it was bigger than he expected and also had more technical equipment.

The final piece of information he was given was a sign-on code for the computer system. He knew that logging in was a risk, because his computer skills were good but not good enough for him to know how to totally erase his visit into the system. But he had no choice—the facility was too big for him to start opening every door and box he found. The online inventory system should tell him what and where immediately.

He started up the computer and typed in the username and passcode. It went blank for several seconds as he held his breath, but then he was presented with a simple and succinct menu. He ran his eyes down the list.

"Bingo," he whispered. There it was: *Eldon specimens – 1977 – 1–22.*

He clicked on the link and was given further lists and codes that he knew would match rooms and areas. He clicked on one of the menu options.

"What the hell?" His brows came together as he read.

- Billy Allison, aged 12 – full transformation
- Adelle Johnson, age 38 – partial transformation
- Max Johnson, age 41 – partial transformation
- Cindy Carol, age 8 – full transformation

There were 22 names overall—most were children, and the adults were either their parents or close relatives.

There was also another list of suspected transformation candidates that numbered in the dozens but a simple tag of *whereabouts unknown* accompanied each.

The first group of eight, oddly called *guests*, were four children and four adults and were housed in Section-F, Room-3. He looked up and saw helpful arrows on walls that indicated which direction that was.

He headed down the black corridor and felt his heart racing as fast as it had done when he was on night-time incursions many years ago. The place was tomb silent and just as dark, and something about it unnerved the hell out of him.

In another few minutes, he found Room-3 and slid the card key down the slot. There was a buzz and a click, and the door popped open. Greg sucked in a deep breath and pushed the door inward.

He stepped inside and the first thing he noticed was that his breath fogged from the cold. The entire room was refrigerated, and from somewhere in the darkness he heard the hum of machines.

Looking around, he couldn't locate a light but moving his flashlight beam, he saw the room was quite large, save for some operating equipment and also a long steel surgical or autopsy table on one side. One wall also had large upright capsules about seven-and-a-half feet tall, with a line of lights on a pad, and what might have been a glass porthole on the upper front.

He crossed to one and shone his light inside but the glass had either stained or become encrusted in grime and he couldn't make out anything inside.

He shone his light down to the hanging clipboard and lifted it to read: *Ainsworth, Martin, male, age 36 – determination: full transmogrification.*

"Transmogrification?" That word was never used in a medical situation and usually meant something changed in a mysterious or even magical way. Johnson Nightbird's warnings of curses rushed back into his mind.

Greg got up on his toes and peered in through the porthole. He then used a sleeve to wipe the exterior and tried again, spending a few seconds trying to see through the grime or condensation on the inside. But still nothing showed.

Down one side were a series of latches, and he put his hand on one. He hesitated but only for a moment because he knew he needed to see, needed his proof. He unlatched the two levers, and with a slight squeal of hinges he drew the heavy lid back, and then stood away a step. There was an escape of a gas cloud, and a smell like spoiled fruit.

"What the fuck?" Inside was completely filled with fibrous growth, like a seven-foot root bundle with a solid core.

Greg couldn't even get his head around what it was supposed to be, but it damned didn't look like anything that was once human. *Was this the end result of the transformation I had seen occurring at the DNA level?* he wondered.

"Weird," he whispered as he carefully closed the door. He left it unlocked because before he left he wanted a sample to take back to analyze.

He went to the next container and read the clipboard's notes: "Cindy Maxwell, aged 11 – *partial transmogrification.*"

He peered in but didn't expect to see anything because if it was a child, they'd be well below the porthole level.

He eased back and then pointed his light down along the row and saw there were over 20 of the coffin-like cylinders. He knew the CDC and them providing such an expansive storage facility meant these things were of interest and also of value. And by the look of their laboratory, they were undoubtedly still examining their samples.

Plus, the autopsy table and invasive medical equipment told him that they were performing both external and internal examinations on their *guests*.

Bottom line, if Cindy was only partially altered, he needed to see her, or what was left of her.

Greg unlatched Cindy's cylinder and pulled the door open. Inside was a smaller body. It was grossly deformed but still vaguely human-shaped and he guessed that was because she was only partially transformed. And still potentially transforming.

He ran the light over her; the child was covered in spidery webbing-like roots and also had thorns, lumps, and bumps sprouting over every inch of exposed skin that was the color of old teak, and even running up through her hair.

Her entire frame looked like old, gnarled bark and he reached out with his flashlight to tap on Cindy's breast—there was a hard *clacking* sound as if he had rapped on a tree stump.

He lifted his gaze to the face, just in time to see the tiny yellow eyes open.

"*Fuck.*"

It, she, Cindy, was still alive. He slammed the door, quickly latching it as something hard like claws skittered against the steel interior.

He shone his light in through the porthole and this time, he could make out frantic movement and a pair of yellow glowing orbs further down.

They're still here, he thought. And still changing. Or *transmogrifying*. Since 1977, they've been kept here, entombed alive in these steel containers.

Greg backed up, knowing he needed to warn Mitch. It was then he heard the slight squeal of hinges again and remembered Martin Ainsworth's isolation chamber was unlocked.

Greg spun but found himself staring at something roughly seven feet tall that was all monstrous plates, tendrils, and thorns, that reached out to take him by the neck.

Thorns pierced his flesh and he beat down on its arm that seemed solid wood and only ended in shredding his own skin from his fists. He was drawn toward the monstrous thing and then horrifyingly, it opened a mouth like a dark hole.

"No, please."

He remembered the last thing Johnson Nightbird had said to him: *curiosity killed the cat*.

CHAPTER 33

Home of Joanne and Gary Adams, parents of James

"That one." Benji pointed. "The one with the big tree in the yard."

"Got it." Mitch pulled in at the manicured streetscape. In the front yard of Number 12 was a pushbike on its side and a football under a huge oak tree.

It was getting late in the afternoon, but as Mitch stepped out, his stomach rumbled as his appetite told him it thought it was dinner time soon even if his watch didn't.

Karen joined him and Benji immediately maneuvered himself to be in front.

"James' parents are Joanne and Gary," Karen said. "I know them, nice couple, and James is an only child."

Mitch was first up onto the porch and knocked on the door. He turned to face Karen and Benji. The boy kept his eyes on the door as though trying to see right through it.

Karen mouthed, *again*.

Mitch did, this time harder.

They saw there was a flicker of movement in the slats of the glass panels in the door and then a shadow appeared there. A soft voice floated through the wooden door. "*Hello*."

"Jo, it's me, Karen. I've got Doctor Mitch Taylor with me." She turned to face Mitch and folded her arms. "We're just following up with a few people on some general community things and, *ah*, it's your turn."

They waited for a full minute but there was no response or movement from the shadow. Karen frowned. "Can you open up, please, Joanne?"

They waited again then finally the latch was slowly drawn back and the inside handle squeaked. The door was pulled inward just a crack. A woman, probably mid-30s, stared out. Mitch noticed that the eye was red-rimmed with a dark circle beneath it.

Karen stepped a little closer. "Joanne, are you okay, honey? Can we come in?"

The eye stared back for a moment more before the door was pulled fully open.

The first thing Mitch noticed was the smell. He turned to Karen, lowering his voice. "Like at the mine site."

Karen went to the woman standing so still in the darkness she might have been an apparition. "Joanne, what is it?"

The woman sucked in a deep breath, held it, as she bit both her lips for a second or two. Her eyes screwed shut as she talked in little more than a squeak. "They're gone."

"Who? James? Is James gone?" Mitch asked.

"And Gary as well." She looked up, but Mitch couldn't see her clearly in the darkness.

"May I?" Mitch didn't wait for approval and quickly reached for the light switch and flicked it on.

The woman cringed, holding her hands over her head as if warding off a blow and keeping her eyes shut tight. That was weird, but it was her appearance that alarmed Mitch most. She had a lumped rash all over her face and her wiry hair looked to be coming out in clumps.

"Oh Joanne." Karen winced but didn't move to touch her. Instead, she pulled Benji back a step, who continued to stare up at the woman with moon-like eyes.

"Mrs. Adams." Mitch gently held the woman's forearms and stared into her face. "Did you go swimming at the mine?"

She shook her head.

"Okay, okay." Mitch continued to stare, but she had lowered her gaze and just seemed defeated. "Where did James and Gary go?"

"James ran away. Then Gary went too." Her throat sounded coarse and painful. She looked up, and Mitch could swear her eyes had a yellow tinge—not the jaundice yellowing of the sclera, but the entire eye.

"Were they sick?" Karen asked.

Joanne seemed to think about it, and then she nodded as her face crumpled. "Yes, very sick. And they...*changed*."

"Has James changed?" Benji frowned in confusion and crept forward. "Into what?"

Karen leaned over to grab his shoulders. "Wait in the car, please. This is important."

"*Aww.*" Benji scowled up at his mother. "But James is my friend, and I know I can help if…"

Karen stared. "*Now.*"

"*Aw-www.*" Benji shook his head and turned. "I get to do nuthin' interesting." He kept muttering all the way outside.

Mitch looked around the house and saw the disheveled state of the place—dirty clothing, food packets, and empty *health tonic* soda bottles colored a brilliant emerald green. He noticed that the clothing Joanne wore was expensive but filthy with sweat and other unidentifiable stains.

"How long have Gary and James been gone?" he asked.

She tilted her head back on her neck and opened her mouth. She swallowed, the action making a hard clicking sound in her throat.

Joanne Adams' head snapped down and she faced him. "Days ago. They're waiting for me." She gritted her teeth, painfully hard, making the cords stand out in her neck.

Karen reached out to her. "Jo, are you okay?"

"It calls." She held a hand to her head. "I can't…"

"Who? What calls?" Mitch ducked his head as he tried to see into her eyes, but she kept them screwed shut.

She started to pull back so Mitch reached for her and grabbed her upper arms, but instead of feeling soft skin, he felt something rough, like tree bark inside her sleeves.

He let her go, remembering Ben Wainright's description of the affliction and also of what he knew had happened to Harlen Bimford.

She tilted her head back. "So deep."

"It's the mine," he said, half-turning to Karen but keeping his eyes on the woman. "Joanne, we need to get you to hospital." He reached for her again. "We'll come back and find James and Gary, we promise."

Her head tilted far back on her neck again and her mouth hung wide. Mitch noticed her throat and teeth looked strange—plus, he could have sworn he saw spikes or thorns in her gullet.

He grabbed hold of her and tried to drag her to the door, but she started to moan and her mouth opened even wider—impossibly wider. He knew the human jaw shouldn't have been able to do that unless it was dislocated.

"It calls. I have to *go-ooo*." She tugged her arm, but Mitch held on.

Karen also reached for her other arm, but then Joanne lunged at Karen, mouth open, and Mitch dragged her back before she could bite. In turn, Joanne rounded on him, jaws snapping.

"Goddamnit, Joanne, stop that!" Karen yelled.

But she kept trying to bite so Mitch pushed her away, and she went to the floor. But she was only down for a moment before she was up and skittering away, on all fours.

She moved fast and unnaturally. Maybe it was the bony extrusions all over her body, but she moved like some sort of hard-shelled insect.

"Jesus, she's having a psychotic episode." He grabbed Karen and pulled her out of the way.

In another moment, there was the crash of breaking glass. Mitch and Karen went after the women but arrived to find the kitchen window broken out and nothing but an empty yard beyond.

"What...what just happened?" Karen blinked several times. "I know Joanne, she's...normal."

"Infected," Mitch said softly.

"Infected? But I thought it was all over." Karen's face creased with anxiety.

"It should be." He turned to her. "The mine is drained."

"It's something else," she said softly.

"There was something." He spun, rushing to the outer room and finding the soda bottle. "This drink, the same one that Harlen had, and we found some residue in the dog's stomach. It's spring water, from underground. Same as like what is bubbling up from the mine—has to be. It's like what Ben Wainright wrote about."

Mitch stared hard at the bottle and remembered seeing this type of soda all over town. "There could be dozens of infected and contagious people wandering around out there."

"Out there?" Karen stared up at him for a moment. "Benji!" She sprinted for the door.

*****

Mitch raced after Karen and arrived in time to see her run around the car, peering in the windows, and screaming her son's name. But there was no one inside, and tellingly, the front passenger door was hanging open.

She turned to him, eyes wide and hands curled into fists. "He's gone. *He's gone!*"

"*Benji!*" Mitch yelled the name and did a broader circle around the car. He tried to remember the details from Wainright's notes. Many of the angel kids were rounded up and taken away, but some were said to have escaped into the countryside and never found. One theory was they entered the mine and went down deep, never to be found again.

"Could he have gone home?" Mitch asked.

"Yes, maybe, but why would he leave us?" She shook her head. "Why would he?"

"James," Mitch replied.

"Yes." She spun to him. "He wanted to help find James. Maybe he went looking for him."

"Or maybe he saw him." Mitch exhaled through pressed lips. "Look, there's a chance, *uh*, that he might have gone to the mine."

Karen slowly turned, her eyes wide. "To the mine—*in* the mine? Why would he?"

"I don't know why, but it's a hunch. It's also where Wainright thought a lot of the missing kids went all those years ago."

She opened the car's front passenger door. "Then that's where we're damn well going. *Now*."

"No, we check your home first to make…"

"*No*, the mine." She bared her teeth in panic.

"And what if he's waiting at home? What if we get trapped somehow and he's left alone?" Mitch reached across to lay a hand on her arm. "It'll take us 10 minutes to swing by your home."

She looked like she was going to explode with impatience before she exhaled in a whoosh. "Okay, okay. Let's go."

Mitch sped so it took them no time to return to Karen's house, and just a single minute more for her to go careening through her place, screaming her son's name.

"Grab another light," Mitch yelled while he stood on the front porch, yelling Benji's name. Karen came barreling out.

"The mine, *go*," was all she said.

"Okay, but call the sheriff. I want someone to know what's going on and where we are." Mitch climbed in as Karen dragged out her phone.

It took them just fifteen minutes to reach the Angel Mine turnoff, and after a few minutes climbing the rutted track, Mitch pulled over and they climbed out.

He reached into his map compartment and retrieved his Glock. He hoped he wouldn't need it, but as the old saying went: better to have it and not need it, than need it and not have it. He also grabbed his flashlight he had remembered to replace.

Karen saw the gun and just nodded. Mitch tucked it into his belt at the small of his back and together they headed up.

At the top of the hill, they stopped.

"It's totally dry," Karen observed.

"Yeah, that's right, all drained away again. Thought it'd be the end of our problems."

Just like what happened back in the 70s, Mitch remembered. *It seemed this stuff bubbles to the surface, infects people, and then goes back to where it came from.*

Mitch stood staring into the impenetrable blackness of the mine mouth where the tainted water had drained away—back to where exactly? And what was in it that caused the infection and alterations in people? He and Greg never really got to the bottom of it.

He'd been a coward to let Mayor Melnick steamroll him against his better judgment, and it made him feel sick to acknowledge it. Well, Melnick be damned, he was sending everything he had off to the CDC, WHO, or anyone else who would listen as soon as he got back.

It was moving to late afternoon now and the shadows were lengthening—and along with them the temperature was dropping. It was still dry, but there was something else different about the site that Mitch couldn't quite put a finger on.

"All those petrified trees are gone," Karen said, frowning. "Someone took them?"

That was it, Mitch thought.

"Maybe," he said, feeling a twist of anxiety begin in his gut.

Mitch wasn't sure when the water had drained, but already the outside ground was dry again, and in the dusty earth were numerous tracks.

"People went into the mine, lots of them," he observed.

Once again, he peered into the charnel darkness of the mine mouth. He didn't want to go in but knew there was no way he wouldn't if there was a chance that Benji was down there somewhere.

Karen cupped her mouth. "Benji!" she yelled and walked a few paces closer to the mine entrance. She sucked in a deep breath. "*Benji-iii*!" This time, it was so loud she went a little hoarse and his name bounced back at her several times before fading into nothingness.

But there was still no reply.

She held her hand out to Mitch. "Give me the flashlight."

"Where's yours?" he asked.

She took the flashlight. "I haven't got one. Only candles." She fished in her pocket. "All I could find was this." She pulled out an old silver cigarette lighter. "Was my ex-husband's."

Mitch groaned. "Okay, give it to me." He took it and tested it, producing a small orange flame.

"He's in there, I can feel it." Her voice trembled.

He nodded to her. "Don't worry. If he is, we'll find him."

Mitch said a silent prayer. And then together they went in.

CHAPTER 34

"Slow down," Mitch demanded.

She ignored him and continued to jog along the tunnel.

In little more than 30 paces, the light from the mouth of the mine suddenly seemed a long way back, and up ahead was nothing but impenetrable darkness. Their only flashlight beam was quickly reduced to a pipe of light that only illuminated a few dozen feet, and Karen had to keep sweeping it from side to side to light their way forward.

The mine was quite large at around seven feet of height, but Mitch still had the urge to crouch.

"Wait up," he said softly, not knowing why he felt the need to whisper. "Point the light at the ground here."

She did as asked, and they saw the footprints—lots of them—coming and going.

"Plenty of traffic," he observed.

"*Shush*." She paused, concentrating, and then slowly shook her head as she faced him. "I can't…there's nothing, not a sound. Maybe they all left." She turned back to the darkness of the seemingly endless tunnel and sucked in a deep breath. "*Benji-iii!*" she yelled.

It made Mitch cringe, and he pulled his gun from behind his back, holding it loosely in his hand.

The echoes bounced back at them for another few seconds until the air dropped to silence again. The pair waited for a few more moments but there was no response.

"Perhaps he's so deep he can't hear us," she said hopefully.

"Yeah, maybe. The footprints go in further," he replied. "We're here now so we should check it out. But best if we're outside for when Sheriff Kehoe arrives."

She nodded and turned back. Mitch noticed the light wobbled in her hands. Oddly, there seemed to be a breeze blowing in their faces, and with it the pervasive smell like from stagnant water—dead fish, methane, and a general slimy rottenness of fetid swamps, toadstools, and dead things that conjured images of a dank shoreline under an eternally black sky.

Mitch thought that maybe they'd find where the water level had retreated to and their way would be blocked. But looking down again, he saw that where they were the ground was already quite dry.

Karen headed off again, and Mitch stayed right on her shoulder. He had that tingling feeling in the back of his neck he used to get on night missions in the forces. But the last time he had it this bad, people died.

Not today, not on his watch, he thought, *and never again.* He pushed the memory down.

"Look." She pointed. "The walls." Karen held the light higher but it was far from steady. Where she illuminated, he could see that the walls were covered in what looked like tree roots. But they were glistening wetly and he had the impression they were like arteries and veins.

"Roots this far down?" she asked.

"It'd need to be a redwood or maybe giant fig tree." Mitch frowned. "Weird." He walked a few paces closer. "Hold the light closer."

She did so.

"They don't look like they're growing down from the surface. But instead up from below." He quickly checked his watch. "Come on, let's keep going a little further."

They continued on a few hundred more feet, and the walls were now totally ribbed by the roots. The silence was suddenly broken by the crunch of feet on gravel.

Mitch lifted his gun and dragged Karen to the side of the mineshaft.

"*Hallooo?*"

He felt relief wash over him. "Sheriff?" Mitch let Karen go and tucked his gun away.

The footsteps got louder, and the tunnel became illuminated by two powerful flashlight beams.

"Doctor Taylor, Vice Mayor." Kehoe touched his hat and thumbed over his shoulder. "Deputy Anderson." The young man with him nodded.

Mitch and Karen quickly updated him on their search and what happened at Joanne and Gary Adams' place. The sheriff's brows knitted ever deeper as he listened.

"Like Buford, and Harlen?" Kehoe's brows went up.

"I hope not, but maybe. Joanne Adams was very sick," Mitch replied.

Kehoe nodded. "And you think that they swam in this bad water and got some sort of mental sickness?" he asked.

Mitch wanted to keep it simple. "Or something they ingested, so maybe it's contagious now, and we need to be careful," he explained.

"What? Shouldn't we be wearing protective clothing?" Deputy Anderson asked.

Mitch was sure the young deputy's blush of pimples on his cheeks just reddened even more.

Mitch shrugged. "I don't know yet. But for now, why don't we just be careful and play it safe by trying not to touch anything down here."

"After what you just told me, that'd be fine if whatever is down here doesn't touch us either." Kehoe hitched his belt and shone his light further down the mineshaft. "Well, let's look for Benji. Deputy Anderson, get up here close by me."

They headed further in and the deeper they went, the more they found that some of the walls had fallen in, exposing entire new tunnels. But these weren't dug by miners and looked more like natural caves. There were also a few huge blocks of stone that had collapsed from the ceiling to the shaft floor.

Mitch stopped and stared at something stuck to the wall.

"What the hell is that?" Kehoe joined him.

"*Yuck.*" Karen spat.

The sheriff lifted his light closer to the foot-long glistening blob stuck to the tunnel wall. It looked like a greasy-black bundle of roots, spreading out in all directions and covered in growths like candy floss and bristled hairs.

But at its center, Mitch could make out a long, thorny mass with a pointed snout at one end.

"I think… I think it's a rat. Or once was." Mitch swallowed down some bile and wondered whether it was Willard, the escapee from his office.

"How…?" Deputy Anderson's voice was reed-thin. "How

did it…?"

Kehoe went to prod it with the flashlight.

"Don't," Mitch said.

"Why?" The sheriff half-turned.

"You heard me when I said don't touch anything down here because it could be infectious, right?" Mitch stepped closer.

Kehoe turned back. "Yeah, yeah, maybe you're right."

They edged around the growth on the wall and continued on for another few minutes. The air was becoming more fetid by the step and the sheriff held up a hand.

"I don't think we can go much further," Kehoe said. "Getting a might dangerous."

"The kids did, and so did some of the adults." Karen pointed down at the ground. "We're not leaving yet."

Kehoe looked one way then the other. "Okay, we'll give it another few hundred feet, but it's a cave-in risk. You can see that too, can't you?" Kehoe didn't wait for an answer.

Karen held up her flashlight, trying to get in front, but after another few minutes they all slowed, becoming more careful as water dripped down on their heads.

"Goddamn stinks in here." Deputy Anderson's nose wrinkled.

"Must be stale air," Kehoe replied.

The air was becoming so thick Mitch could almost taste it now. As they crossed by an alcove, Karen screamed and fell against him. Her light went haywire for a moment and Mitch grabbed her arm to steady it while also drawing his weapon.

In the side tunnel that had broken open, perhaps by the force of the water, stood one of the petrified statues. Karen held her wobbly light on it for a moment.

"What is that thing doing down here?" She looked briefly up at him, her breathing coming fast.

Mitch lowered his gun. "I don't think it's like the ones from outside."

Kehoe glanced at Mitch's gun for a moment and grunted his displeasure. Mitch ignored him, took the flashlight from Karen, and went a little closer. He was right; it was and wasn't like the ones outside. This one was wet-looking and the features more distinct. He briefly shone his light at the cave ceiling to see if water was dripping on it but found the rest of the cavern fairly dry.

He brought the light back to the thing's head—undoubtedly, this one was a work of art, and if not for the rough wooden surface, was absolutely lifelike.

Oddly, the roots were twined around it, growing up from the floor and embracing it. The other difference was instead of having a visage of agony, the face of this petrified statue made it look like the subject was in ecstasy.

"Amazing," Kehoe whispered. "Did someone bring this down here, or was it always here?"

Karen came closer. "It looks like it's growing down here. How is that possible?"

"Or taken root," Kehoe said.

"Was this here before? Does anyone know?" Mitch asked.

Kehoe shrugged. "Never been this far in. Never had a reason to."

Karen went up to the thing and peered into the upturned face. "It seems, almost, familiar." She held up a hand. "I could swear it looks like Marshal Simmons, the garage owner."

Kehoe squinted. "Yeah, it does look a little like old Marsh."

"Simmons is on our missing person's list, boss," Deputy Anderson said softly.

Karen reached up with her flashlight to prod at the statue. "Hard, but not quite petrified hard."

Kehoe shone his light around at the walls. "Those damn roots are everywhere."

Mitch followed his gaze; Karen and Deputy Anderson did the same.

"No more statues. Thank God." She turned her light back to the single statue. "Just this one…*hey!*"

Mitch spun back.

"Has this thing…?" She turned to Mitch, frowning.

Mitch knew what she was getting at. The statue's face seemed to have turned a fraction. Before, it was tilted up toward the cave ceiling but now was slightly angled toward them.

"Please tell me it's just a trick of the light." Deputy Anderson's voice was strained.

Mitch felt a tingle run up his spine. Kehoe's light went from the thing's head down to it base, and he saw that it also seemed to have slid along the ground.

"Yeah, I'm thinking we should probably leave now." Kehoe lifted his light to the statue's face.

Its eyes flicked open.

"*Shit*." Mitch lifted his gun.

The twin orbs were a brilliant yellow and shone like lights in the darkness. Then to everyone's horror, it screamed, a sound so animalistic and ear-piercing it stretched their nerves to breaking.

"*It's freaking alive*!" Kehoe yelled.

With the sound of ripping root-threads, it took a step toward them and its arm rose.

"*Move, move, move*!" Mitch yelled.

Deputy Anderson was first out of the side cave, followed by Mitch dragging Karen with him. Kehoe came last while keeping his gun trained on the thing.

Out in the main shaft, Kehoe headed toward the exit, but Karen sprinted to get in front of him. Mitch tried to stop her.

"No." She swiped Mitch's hand away. "We are *not* leaving without my son."

"We need backup," Kehoe said. "This is beyond us."

As Mitch, Kehoe, and Karen debated their next move, from behind them came a gurgling noise, and Mitch spun to see the deputy being held by another of the statues.

Kehoe and Mitch raised their guns, but the thing had the deputy between itself and the line of fire.

"Get out of the way!" Kehoe yelled, his gun up and steady.

Karen shrunk back but toward the cave depths. As they watched, the statue thing leaned forward to fix its mouth to Anderson's neck and as the young man screamed, the hard thorn-encrusted lips burrowed in.

"*No shot, no shot!*" Kehoe screamed. "Anderson, get out of the fucking way."

Mitch didn't have a clear shot either but fired anyway. His bullet struck the side of the thing's head, blasting away a fist-sized piece of the lumped, overgrown skull.

Even after the damage, it didn't let go and in the glare of the light, its eyes fixed on him and he could see inside the open skull was just a mad tangle of what looked like fibrous roots.

It took its mouth off the young man's neck long enough to bare thorn-like teeth coated in blood. Mitch fired twice more. This time, most of the top of the head, from nose up, was blown clean away.

Even with the top half of its head gone, the thing didn't go down. Instead, it dropped the deputy and stumbled away into the darkness as Karen screamed behind them. Kehoe rushed to Anderson as he fell, holding his neck as blood pulsed through his fingers.

"Gotta get him out." Kehoe lifted his deputy.

Mitch spun to where Karen had been. She was gone.

*****

"Karen!" Mitch shouted. "*Karen*!" He roared again and then jogged a few paces further in.

"Goddamnit," Kehoe said between clamped teeth. He shook his head and exhaled. "Sorry, Mitch, got to get my deputy topside before he bleeds out."

Mitch half-turned. "Go." But then spun back to the sheriff. "Wait." He ran to snatch the deputy's large black flashlight from his belt.

Kehoe held his deputy under his arm, and then nodded to Mitch. "Good luck, son."

"You too. Both of you," Mitch replied. "See you soon."

*,kh.hk***

Mitch went fast, holding the gun out in front of him and the flashlight underneath, trying to cover every inch of the mineshaft.

In the cave, the tree roots were everywhere now, like ribbing, and making the shaft seem more like the gullet of a large animal. Several times, he came across the standing statues, and even though some slowly turned on creaking necks to watch him pass, none moved from where they had taken root.

He now knew this was what was happening to many of the people who were infected. Perhaps to begin with they were just feral creatures like Benji's friend James, but once they made it to the mine, many began to complete their transformation.

And the others? He wondered whether the other people who had disappeared were changed or snatched and brought down here? He just hoped they weren't killed immediately, giving him a chance to save Benji and Karen.

From out of the darkness, something flew at him and struck his chest and stuck there. It immediately tried to burrow its sharp, pointed head into him, and he grabbed at it, immediately spiking his hands on all the thorns and sharp edges jutting from its hard body.

Thorny wings flapped on the thing and he threw it hard onto the ground and stamped a large boot on it, making it break like a crustacean's shell and spilling its mushy, fibrous contents to the floor.

Was that a bird once? he wondered.

There was more flapping and then another came at him, flying awkwardly as it tried to keep its ungainly size and shape in the air. Mitch took no chances this time and quickly lifted the gun, fired once, and blew the thing out of the air. It landed in a brittle heap to the mine floor and lay still.

"It's a damn madhouse," he whispered, his chest now pumping hard.

He ran on, gathering speed, and after another 20 minutes, he stopped to drag in lungfuls of putrid air and just listen. There was the sound of water up ahead, and after a moment thinking through the pros and cons of making any noise, he decided.

"*Karen?*" his voice boomed and then echoed away from him. He was about to call again when a tiny scream came back—*it was her*—and Mitch launched himself forward, sprinting now.

After another few hundred feet, the rotting, fishy smell took on a more distinct odor. He'd smelled it before—the eggy odor of methane gas.

Mitch slowed as the tunnel became wetter and even more thickly malodorous. The walls were moving now almost in peristaltic waves like the inside of a gut. He felt like he was being swallowed alive and soon to be digested.

The tunnel had ended, and he moved through raw tumbled rock, obviously where the miners had accidentally broken through into the water cavern all those decades ago. He had to breathe shallowly, as the gas was starting to make his head and vision swim.

Mitch eased through a crack in the rock face and crawled out into a large cavern that, due to its size, seemed to have no end. Where he emerged, he found he was up high and looking down on a dark lake of bubbling liquid. The methane gas was percolating up from below to pop in little explosions of green vapor from its surface.

He stood with his mouth hanging open, astounded and probably dealing with shock as he stared—hundreds of feet out from the shoreline was some sort of island and on it was a single massive tree-like thing. And it moved. Because it was alive.

"*Adotte Sakima*," Mitch softly said the name of the first people's powerful god.

"It's real," he whispered.

As he stared, he saw that the roots of the monstrosity constantly shifted, snaking about and curling over objects that it snatched up and fed into itself. Hanging from its withered branches were pendulous bulbs like hideous fruits that writhed and jiggled and threatened to birth hideous things.

The primitive core of his mind rebelled at the horror and screamed for him to turn and flee, but his military training forced him to stand firm and face it down. He had been in hair-raising situations before, but those times it was human monsters he had to deal with, and now it was something from an ancient time of dark nightmare.

But above it all, he knew Karen and Benji were down there somewhere, and he would never leave without them.

"I'll never lose anyone again," he said to strengthen his own resolve.

Mitch felt light-headed from the methane-laden air but still slid down the slope, holding his light up. The powerful beam only just reached to the island, but he saw there were bodies floating in the disgusting water, some face down, but others being dragged out toward the waiting tree—no, not bodies…people, as some of them still feebly struggled. It was these poor souls that the roots delicately picked from the water and stuffed into one of many red-lined orifices on the mighty trunk.

"*Ah* shit," Mitch whispered. This was the thing the Paleo Indians had tried to warn them about all those millennia ago. Those carvings and painted images in caves were of this tree god, the *Adotte Sakima*, that lived below them all.

Mitch wondered whether it was some freak of nature, a mutation, or even if it originated from this world at all. And how many thousands of years ago had the waters first surged to the surface and its seeds infected people or grew inside them then turning them into some sort of quasi-plant beings to do the bidding of a living, sentient tree? The rest of the people were captured and herded down here to be nothing more than living plant food.

"*Karen*!" he yelled again.

"Mitch!"

His head swung to the voice and he saw her then. A group of the petrified-looking beings dragged several people toward the water. Karen was there, clinging to a smaller body, which lifted his spirits a fraction to know it was undoubtedly Benji—she had found her son and done what she set out to do.

He reached for his gun but realized he could never fire it in here now as he might ignite the methane gas. So instead, he began to run toward them, now not having any plan at all.

As he did, the branches of the tree stopped their sinuous movement as though the massive growth finally became aware of him.

In seconds more, from the fetid lake, from the walls, and lifting from the rotten earth, strange figures began to rise up. If they had once been people, they were nothing like that now. Instead, they were decrepit creatures with twisted limbs, spiked growths or wing-like extrusions branching from them, and glowing yellow eyes with bodies all held together by slimy mosses and meshes of fibrous vein-like roots.

They screeched and whined and scuttled toward him. Some hobbled on broken limbs, some dragged themselves trailing fibrous roots, but others came incredibly fast.

Mitch began to run toward Karen and Benji, and as he closed in on them, he lowered his shoulder and charged one of the beings holding onto her. He struck it hard and knocked it backward a dozen feet, but it damn hurt and felt like he had just rammed a tree trunk.

Mitch used the only weapon he had—the heavy Maglite flashlight—and he swung it like a club, smashing it down and crunching away chunks of the petrified skin and caving-in heads.

In seconds more, he had freed them, but only temporarily as hundreds of the things were coming at them fast.

"Can you run?" he asked her.

She clung to him and nodded jerkily.

"And Benji?" He lifted the boy's chin. Benji nodded more slowly and it seemed the methane was fogging his mind after being down here so long. It would happen to all of them soon, and then they'd either be fed to the tree god or changed to become its servants until they eventually rotted down to nothing.

"Gotta move, Benji. We have to run fast, and you must keep up with your mom, okay?"

Benji nodded again and put a hand on Mitch's shoulder to lift himself to his feet. He opened glassy eyes wider.

"I dreamed you'd both come get me, Batman." He gave them a hazy smile. "I want to go home now."

Mitch helped Karen up and then turned to the approaching horde. He knew they'd never be able to outrun them all.

"I'm going to slow them down." He handed her the gun. "Use this, but *do not* fire it until you're out of this cavern. And *don't* stop running for anything, okay?"

"No, not without you." Her eyes were panicked.

"I'll be right behind you. Don't stop for anything. Go! Save your son." Mitch pushed her. "*Save Benji.*"

Her face was twisted with anguish, but she nodded and then the pair began a staggered run to the mouth of the cavern.

Mitch turned back toward the horrifying beings that were coming at them. He felt his stomach roil with fear as it looked like someone had opened the gates of Hell as they came toward him. To his horror, he saw that some began to run toward Karen and Benji, trying to head them off.

He waved his light at them. "*Hey*! Here I am, you ugly bastards."

He bent to pick up a slimy stone and hoisted it at the group, managing to strike one, but it didn't even flinch. He picked up another rock and this time threw it with all his might toward the tree. It fell short, sending up a splash of mucousy water. But even the failed attempt prompted a response to his attack on their god. Immediately, all the things turned toward him. And only him.

"Here it comes." He ground his teeth together hard to stop his chin from shaking and then, turning, saw that Karen and Benji had vanished back out through the crack in the wall. He began to edge backward. Unfortunately, there were so many, he knew that they'd cut him off before he made it to the opening.

From high above, he saw that those branching things on the back had purpose, as some flapped the membranous coral-like wings to swoop down on him. He turned back to see there was even worse news—some of the horrors were running a lot faster than Karen could manage and she'd be chased down before they reached the surface.

"Never lose anyone again," he breathed out. His mind was becoming foggy from the gas and his thinking clouded. Flashbulbs of light began to go off behind his eyes and he suddenly remembered another woman who had died in his place on the battlefields of Syria, seeming like 100 years ago.

"Not this time, you sonofabitch."

He smiled as he reached into his pocket for the cigarette lighter, drew it out, and held it up. He looked out toward the grotesque tree and saw that it had gone back to feeding human beings, some struggling, into the many maws along its trunk. It obviously felt it had won.

"Go to Hell." Mitch flicked the lighter's tiny wheel.

CHAPTER 35

Karen staggered toward the mouth of the mineshaft, dragging her son with her. From up ahead, she could hear a voice chanting, and as she emerged, there was an ancient Native American to the side with his arms raised and eyes closed.

"Help us," she begged.

But he ignored her and continued to chant his words in a sing-song manner and stamped his feet. Next to him was a smoking pile of shrubs that gave off an odor of eucalyptus, licorice, and other fragrant scents.

He stopped his chant and turned ancient eyes on her. "Hurry now, move away. Retribution is coming."

Karen sucked in a huge breath and dragged Benji forward. There was no one else waiting for them, as the sheriff had obviously taken his deputy to hospital.

Benji wheezed as he recovered from the methane saturation in his lungs. Karen pull-lifted him out of the small depression in front of the mine mouth, just as she felt the ground rumble beneath her feet. In another second, an orange hurricane burst from the shaft to roar like a jet engine and incinerate the remaining twisted trees and everything else before it.

She threw Benji down and covered him with her body but luckily, she was to the side of the gout of flame. After another minute, she slowly sat up, her eyes glistening as she realized what it meant.

Benji coughed. "Where's Mitch?"

She blinked as he stared into the mine. "He stayed…" she whispered, "…to save us."

"I knew he would," Benji said.

"It's over," the old man said. "I beat it."

"*You* beat it?" She shook her head. "Mitch saved us."

Johnson Nightbird grunted softly, and then turned back to the smoking shaft. "But it was me that called him to save

Eldon." He faced her. "And you."

Karen wiped her eyes and stared back at the mineshaft. The flames were dying down, but there was still an orange glow coming from deep down in the mine's throat that made it look like the entrance to Hell.

"Thank you, Mitch," she whispered. "Thank you for saving us."

EPILOGUE

Minneapolis, Minnesota – Population 453,325

"What have we got here? Desmond Morrison was President of Landers Supermarket Chain that had stores in every state, bar Alaska. And he was working on that."

He looked at the crate of emerald green bottles—Eldon Spring Water—Super Health Tonic was printed on the label in stylized green calligraphy and blazed across images of a crystal-clear lake, waterfall, and trees with colorful birds. *Eye catching*, he thought.

Danny Barker lifted a bottle free and cradled it in his hand. "It's the next big thing, and free samples for our new customers. It tastes great and contains no caffeine, sugar, or artificial flavorings. Natural mineral-infused water from the pristine underground lakes of Eldon. With just a hint of lemon zest." He held it out. "Try it."

Desmond eyed him suspiciously for a moment and then took it, twisted the cap off, and sniffed. He seemed to approve as he tilted it to his lips and firstly sipped, but then kept going until half was gone.

Danny worked to suppress his shark-smile as he knew he had him. In sales, it was called *getting the prospect to take ownership*.

"We're only doing 100,000 units per day, so numbers are limited for now." He shrugged. "It's a little more expensive than our usual products, but I think you'll agree it's well worth it."

Desmond lowered the bottle and looked at the label for a moment more. "The next big thing, *huh*?"

"Bigger than goji berries and coconut water combined. And only available from Eldon Spring Water Company." He grinned and waited.

"Volume discount?" Desmond raised his chin.

Danny's face became serious. "Not really, but for you, I can knock off two percent if you take 10,000."

"Five," Desmond countered.

Danny shook his head. "Demand is already too high; three percent, best I can do. And that's only if you take 15,000 units."

Desmond eyeballed him for a moment, but then stuck his hand out. "Done. Organize the paperwork."

"You got it." Danny gave him a firm *I-mean-business* handshake. Truth was, he'd closed every deal today with the new drink. It was proving a big mover, and the test run they'd done in the hometown of Eldon had shown an overwhelming approval rating. *Eat your heart out, Candy Cola*, he thought.

"I want it on the shelves first thing Monday morning." Desmond got to his feet. "Let's make everyone in the country as healthy as they are in Eldon."

"That's the plan," Danny replied, as he surreptitiously scratched at the strange pebbly rash on his arm.

END

SEVEREDPRESS

@severedpress
/severedpress

Checkout other great books by bestselling author
Greig Beck

PRIMORDIA: IN SEARCH OF THE LOST WORLD

Ben Cartwright, former soldier, home to mourn the loss of his father stumbles upon cryptic letters from the past between the author, Arthur Conan Doyle and his great, great grandfather who vanished while exploring the Amazon jungle in 1908. Amazingly, these letters lead Ben to believe that his ancestor's expedition was the basis for Doyle's fantastical tale of a lost world inhabited by long extinct creatures. As Ben digs some more he finds clues to the whereabouts of a lost notebook that might contain a map to a place that is home to creatures that would rewrite everything known about history, biology and evolution. But other parties now know about the notebook, and will do anything to obtain it. For Ben and his friends, it becomes a race against time and against ruthless rivals. In the remotest corners of Venezuela, along winding river trails known only to lost tribes, and through near impenetrable jungle, Ben and his novice team find a forbidden place more terrifying and dangerous than anything they could ever have imagined.

THE FOSSIL

Klaus and Doris have just made the discovery of their lives – a complete Neanderthal skeleton buried in a newly opened sinkhole. But on removing it, something else tumbles free. Something that switches on, and then calls home.Soon the owners are coming back, and nothing will stop their ruthless search for their lost prize. Gruesome corpses begin to pile up, and Detective Ed Heisner of the Berlin Police is assigned to a case like nothing he has ever experienced before in his life. Heisner must stay one step ahead of a group of secretive Special Forces soldiers also tracking the strange device, while trying to find an unearthly group of killers that are torturing, burning, and obliterating their victims all the way across the city.THE FOSSIL is a time jumping detective novella where humans soon find that time can be the greatest weapon of all.*
THE FOSSIL first appeared in SNAFU No.1 (2014) as a short story. Due to numerous requests, it has now been expanded and released here in its complete, stand-alone novella form.

SEVEREDPRESS

@severedpress
/severedpress

Checkout other great books by bestselling author
Greig Beck

TO THE CENTER OF THE EARTH

An old woman locked away in a Russian asylum has a secret—knowledge of a 500-year-old manuscript written by a long-dead alchemist that will show a passage to the mythical center of the Earth.She knows it's real because 50 years ago, she and a team traveled there. And only she made it back. Today, caving specialist Mike Monroe leads a crew into the world's deepest cave in the former Soviet Union. He's following the path of a mad woman, and the words of an ancient Russian alchemist, that were the basis of the fantastical tale by Jules Verne.But what horrifying things he finds will tear at his sanity and change everything we know about evolution and the world, forever.In the tradition of Primordia, Greig Beck delivers another epic retelling of a classic story in an electrifying and terrifying adventure that transcends the imagination."Down there, beyond the deepest caves, below the crust and the mantle, there is another world."

THE SIBERIAN INCIDENT

100,000 years ago the object hit the lake at the deepest point, quickly sinking into its mile-deep stygian darkness. With it came something horrifying that would threaten every living thing on the face of the planetOver the centuries, legends grew of people vanishing, of strange, deformed animals, and of an unexplained luminescence down in the lake depths.When Marcus Stenson won the lucrative contract to create a sturgeon fish farm on the site of disused paper mill on the shore of Lake Baikal, he thought he had hit the jackpot. He refused to listen to the chilling folktales, or even be concerned by the occasional harassment from the local mafia. But then animals were found mutilated in the frozen forest, and people started to go missing. And worse, some came back, changed, horribly.In the depths of the lake, something unearthly that had been waiting 100,000 years was stirring. And mankind will become nothing more than a host.THE SIBERIAN INCIDENT - a tale of invasive Alien Horror from international best selling author, Greig Beck.

Printed in Dunstable, United Kingdom